LOST *in* SIERRA

IN THE SAME BOAT

LOST *in* SIERRA

DIANA VAZQUEZ

COTEAU BOOKS

WWW.COTEAUBOOKS.COM

This novel is a work of fiction. Names, characters, places, and incidents either are the product of the author's imagination or are used fictitiously. Any resemblance to actual persons, living or dead, is coincidental.

Editor for the Series, Barbara Sapergia.
Edited by Geoffrey Ursell.
Cover painting and interior illustrations by German Jaramillo.
Cover and book design by Duncan Campbell.
"In The Same Boat" logo designed by Tania Wolk, Magpie Design.
Printed and bound in Canada by Houghton-Boston, Saskatoon.

National Library of Canada Cataloguing in Publication Data

Vazquez, Diana.
Lost in Sierra

ISBN 1-55050-184-4

I. Title.
PS8593.A988L67 2001   JC813'.54 C2001-911225-4
PZ7.V396LO 2001

10 9 8 7 6 5 4 3 2 1

COTEAU BOOKS
401-2206 Dewdney Ave.
Regina, Saskatchewan
Canada   S4R 1H3

AVAILABLE IN THE US FROM
General Distribution Services
4500 Witmer Industrial Estates
Niagara Falls, NY,   14305-1386

The publisher gratefully acknowledges the financial assistance of the Saskatchewan Arts Board, the Canada Council for the Arts, including the Millennium Arts Fund, the Government of Canada through the Book Publishing Industry Development Program (BPIDP), and the City of Regina Arts Commission, for its publishing program.

PREFACE

JANET LUNN

"WHY AREN'T THERE ANY STORIES ABOUT US?" has been a heartfelt cry of Canadian children not descended from either French or English forebears for too long. In recent years, writers like Paul Yee, Leo Yerxa, Shizuye Takashima, and William Kurelek have created beautiful picture books and retellings of folk tales from the cultures of their ancestors. But there have been almost no children's novels, no up-to-date stories with which these children might identify.

Not more than a generation ago, this was true for all Canadian children. All but a small handful of their books came from Great Britain, France, or the United States. That is certainly not true now. Canadian children can immerse themselves happily in stories set in their own towns and countrysides, identify with characters like themselves, and be comforted and bolstered by a shared experience. This is what children of Japanese or African or indigenous North American descent have been wanting to do.

This series, In the Same Boat, was motivated by the desire of Coteau Books to do something about this. What a good idea it was! In these first five books for readers in their middle years of childhood, five writers, from five different backgrounds, offer the children who share these backgrounds stories in which they can recognize themselves and the way they live. At the same time, they offer all children insights into these diverse cultures.

These are five good stories, strong works of fiction, but what is perhaps more important is that they are all told honestly and with the authority that is only given to writers who truly understand what they are writing about.

*To my mother and father,
and to my brother, Sandy.*

ONE

FROM THE WINDOW OF THE AIRPLANE I COULD SEE THE sun send a hot orange line across a sky that looked like lava. Then we descended into a blanket of thick, dark clouds, and before I knew it, rain streaked across the windows. I couldn't see anything outside except grey fog. After seven hours, I was finally arriving at my destination: Spain.

The plane seemed to hang motionless in the clouds, and its quiet rumbling made me yawn and close my eyes. Why had I been sent here? Because my *abuela,* my grandmother, who'd been my protector and champion, whose shop had been my safe haven, had sent me out into the world by myself.

Abuela had a store on College Street called *Sol de España,* where I went every day after school. When I was there nothing bothered me. In fact, I didn't even care that

"Marky" (Mark Stevens, the school bully) lived a few doors down. There were times, of course, when it was a definite disadvantage, like when he'd had a bad day and was looking to take it out on someone who happened to be walking home the same way.

I'd have to use my escape route then: through the backyards along Manning, over the wall behind Perreiro's pharmacy, and down the laneway. I was smaller and faster going through the loose fence boards before the lane and I gained a second over him. But when we went over the wall behind the pharmacy, I had to scramble across it and usually banged my knees, while Marky took it in one muscular leap. Then there was the final dash down the laneway where I could hear him gaining on me. Just in range of his fingertips, I'd round the corner and soar in front of Abuela's shop window, my arms in the air as if I was breaking a ribbon at the finish line. I'd stumble into the safety of her store and lie gasping on the floor.

"Bravo!" my grandmother, Abuela, and her regular customers always greeted me. "Ana, the Olympian!"

"Ana, champion of everything."

My fan club.

Señor Julio, with his pencil-thin moustache and pressed suit, always jumped up to open the door for me when they saw me round the corner, and would stand holding the doorknob, like a most cultivated butler. He'd glance at his watch. *"Tres minutos y veinte seis segundos despues de las cuatro, Señorita Ana!* Three minutes and twenty-six seconds after four, Miss Ana. How did you ever make it here so quickly!? You are growing wings on your feet."

I'd watch Marky saunter by the window. I could never admit to Abuela and her friends that I was running away from him. "I'm still practising for the track team at school," I'd manage to gasp.

My first unlucky encounter with Marky occured when I'd been chosen to hand around a plate of cookies in class. I'd gone up and down the rows, enjoying my momentary popularity, until there were only two cookies left. My happiness ended abruptly when someone stuck their foot out just as I was coming up to Marky's desk. I fell forward, and the plate of cookies smashed on the ground. When I looked up, Marky's unforgiving eyes met mine.

I don't know if it was nerves or bad luck, but I was always a klutz around him. There was the time I was returning to my seat from the bathroom and he was reaching for a pencil he'd just dropped. I stepped on his fingers and felt the pencil snap under my shoe. There was the time I opened a door just as he rounded a corner and he walked into it. Freak accidents. We never talked about things. I always said, "I'm sorry." And he always said, "You're dead."

I was a skinny, pale kid. But I had a good jaw. I could stick it out and make it look square like the amazing jaws the superheroes had in the comic books. For a very brief time, I believed I had superhuman strength too. I confided my secret to Abuela and she agreed with me. But when school started, I figured out that I was better at running away from evil than fighting it. It was a crushing disappointment to realize I wasn't hero material. Abuela still told everyone I could wrestle a tidal wave to the ground if I wanted to. And part of me secretly thought that if she kept believing it, it might come true some day.

Abuela's crowded store was full of souvenirs from Spain: painted fans, fancy soaps, castanets, and posters of bullfighters and flamenco dancers. Abuela had two regular customers, short, plump Señora Carol, and the extremely polite Señor Julio. They were there every day, sitting by the counter and reading the newspaper or chatting with Abuela. She didn't have a lot of customers, but people did come in to buy the fresh sausages she had delivered to her store. She always ordered too much, and my family ended up eating sausages for dinner at least twice a week.

In the winter when it was too dark and cold to play outside, Señor Julio set up a chessboard and taught me how to play. Once when he got up to sing a *zarzuela* with Abuela and Señora Carol, I moved twice. He came back to the table and studied the board, "Don't move twice,

Ana. You'll lose twice as fast."

"What do you know, old man?" Abuela said, switching to conversation in mid-song: *"...there's a girl in a dress of lavender...*in a year she'll chase you around that board."

"I have no doubt, Consuelo," Señor Julio bowed, remaining polite even when teased, "if she is graced with the intelligence and wit of her grandmother."

"If?! Just look at her. She's a miracle, a gift!" Abuela came over and kissed my face until I protested loudly.

But our favourite game was the hiding game. Señor Julio called it "Detective". They hid things and made me find them. At first it took me a long time to find the peanuts or toffees they hid, but when I figured out their secrets, I found everything. All I needed to know was who had hidden the treasure. Señor Julio's eyes always crept over to his hiding spot, so I just sat and watched him until his eyes gave it away. Señora Carol was almost as short as I was so she hid everything in low places, or under things. Abuela was the hardest to figure out, because half the time she was talking while she hid things and didn't even remember herself where she put them. Once I found my treasure in the fridge with the sausages.

The only place no one *ever* hid anything was in the basement. Everyone knew it was dark in the basement. And my fear of darkness was so big, I couldn't even hide it from my fan club. I would stand up to a thousand

Markys before I ever went down into the basement.

As I got older and Marky stopped chasing me, the detective game became bigger. Abuela and her friends would leave me in the store and huddle out on the sidewalk to plan where they would hide things. Sometimes the treasures weren't even in the store. Señora Carol taped things under the bench by the streetcar stop; Señor Julio liked to hide things in the open, like on the window ledge outside the store, or behind a drainspout. If I was patient, they eventually gave me a clue, sometimes just in their conversation. They kept saying they were going to hide things far from downtown, in Etobicoke or Scarborough, and make me try to find them.

I urged them to do it, which made Abuela laugh, but one day she looked at me thoughtfully and said she had lost something very special in Spain and she was going to send me back there to find it. When I asked her what it was, she waved the question away. "It was a long time ago."

"I would find it for you, Abuela."

"I know, Ana," she said and folded me in her arms. "Maybe one day you will go to Spain and find what I have waited all my life for."

"What is it, Abuela?"

But she didn't want to tell me. "When you are older, I will tell you. Today, I am a tired old woman." Her black hair wasn't as neatly tucked into a bun as it usually was, and I noticed the grey strands falling over her face. She looked old. "Promise you'll tell me soon?" I whispered.

"I will."

"Tomorrow?"

"Soon." She patted my hand and sent me home. I would have stayed with her if I'd known she was sick. But even Abuela didn't know she was sick. She only felt tired, so very tired.

ABUELA'S WILL WAS FULL OF SURPRISES. She left her favourite things to my mother: old family recipes that she had put in a book marked SECRET!, and her small, colourful apartment. She left her store, *Sol de España,* to her regular customers, Señor Julio and Señora Carol. And to me she left a ticket to Spain.

I didn't want to go to Spain. I wanted to stay in Toronto and play hide-and-seek in the laneways. I wanted to run barefoot through sprinklers and go to the corner store for popsicles and walk back up the street, looking at everyone on their front porches. Besides, I had just turned thirteen and I was finally allowed to go to the movies alone with my friends. There was so much to look forward to in the summer, but it was Abuela's last wish that I go to Spain, and my mother thought a change would be good for everyone.

The year wasn't going well. My father had lost his job and was spending a lot of time hanging around at home. He'd started expecting me to take on the world. Everything suddenly counted, every little chore had to be done just right, every game that I didn't try my best at was a big deal, every test that I didn't ace was a disaster. Then, out of the blue, he wanted me to take up boxing.

"What've you got to lose, Ana, eh? Come on, it'll be great! Give you confidence, put some bite in you. Don't think I haven't been watching you – you don't stand up for yourself. You've got to learn to do that, or people will walk all over you. *Believe me, I know.*" He was saying that a lot now. As if he'd learned something the rest of the world still didn't know.

I could tell it mattered a lot to him, so I went down the street to Mack's Gym to see what the lessons were like. When I came home with a program, I found him on the porch jabbing at a forsythia bush that leaned over the railing, and I wondered why he didn't take lessons himself.

My first sparring partner, Ashley, was built like the trunk of a tree – very round and straight. And strong. She got annoyed when I tried to lighten the mood in the ring with a few jokes, and pushed me up against the ropes until the coach pulled her off. The sessions always ended with two-minute matches when Ashley pummelled her way through the girls in the class until she was the last one unbeaten.

At the end of the course, we had a championship meet. I was the third one up. I knew the order would satisfy my father, who I could see sitting close to the front. He would take it to mean that I wasn't the very worst. I wondered if he'd notice that the girls ahead of me were eight years old. When my turn came, my father leaned back in a pose of relaxation. He couldn't hold it long, though, and as I moved into the centre of the ring, he came up to the edge of his seat. Undefeated, Ashley waited for me. We touched gloves and brought our hands up in front of our faces. I jumped back from her first bear swipe and circled, giving her a wide berth. My father was distracting me, shadow boxing in his seat, his eyes zapping me with messages.

I saw two red globes come at me. One, two. I was cuffed on the bottom lip. It felt as if my lip was torn off. I did a kangaroo jump back while I tried to figure out how to lose without getting killed.

Ashley came towards me to finish it off, bouncing on her feet and jabbing out quickly. I ducked and glanced at my father. There shining out of his face was all the hope and fear in the world. My stomach did a flip that travelled all the way up to my throat and made me feel like crying. I had to get at least one punch in for him. Family honour and all that.

I hopped away from Ashley, who hissed at me to stay

put. I let her follow me around the ring, then jumped forward suddenly, the element of surprise in my favour. My punch landed right in the middle of her forehead. She staggered back, her eyes and mouth open in surprise. It was comical – supremely comical. I stumbled to the ground, laughing. Through my watering eyes, I could see three globes perched above me – Ashley's gloves and her red face. She was about to dive on me and end it all when the referee intervened and we were sent to our corners.

Round two. I had never made it to the second round. My father was making his way towards me with a bagful of coaching tips. Thankfully, the bell rang and I only faintly heard him yell, *"Don't laugh when you punch her!"*

Ashley came out with an ugly intensity. Robo-bear. I wondered how much it would hurt to die. My father was up on the edge of his seat, weaving and boxing with new energy. A cuff landed on the side of my head. I stumbled back, and her follow-up punch slid past me. I bounced on my toes, waiting for her to come at me again. I just wanted to be somewhere else now. My father was punching the air, his fists getting close to the people in the row in front of him. The more I looked at him, the more furiously he jabbed at the air and waved my attention back to the fight. My father made contact with the head in front of him just as Ashley planted a punch between my eyes.

Through an explosion of pain and shooting stars, I could see my father being lifted out of his seat by a burly man – Ashley's father, I think – then I fell on the deck and the ring faded into darkness.

THE PLANE CAME OUT OF THE LOW CLOUDS and touched the runway, jolting me back to my arrival in Spain. I stepped out of the plane onto the tarmac, and the smell of diesel fuel filled the air. A small bus was waiting to take us to the terminal, where we went through passport control. My parents' instructions were crumpled in my pocket. I pulled them out. My mother had written most of the instructions in her neat handwriting, and my father had inserted comments in his big scrawl.

Hello Sweetie,

You're sitting on the plane now. (I wasn't. I had opened the letter once I'd passed passport control in Canada, thinking if there were any nasty surprises I would bolt back.) *I can't believe you're going away for the whole summer, but I know this will be a wonderful experience. MAKE THIS COUNT, SUGAR.*

There were some last-minute problems with your transportation to Sierra, but don't worry, someone

will come and pick you up. Just stay by the gate.
DON'T TALK TO STRANGERS. (Of course this is impos-
sible in a country where you know no one – but you
know what your father means. Be street-smart.)
DON'T LET ANYONE RIP YOU OFF – BARTER IN THE
MARKETPLACES – YOU'RE A DESCENDANT!

Be careful, be safe, and have a great trip. We miss
you already. ADIOS, DARLING. We'll see you at the end
of the summer.

Love, Mom and Dad
PS. Try the churros. They're great!

I looked around. No one paid attention to me. The passengers had dispersed, and I was left standing alone by the gate. Outside all I could see was grey concrete. It didn't look like the mythical land that Abuela used to talk about: *The skies stay powder blue all the way up to the stars.* *The olive trees are hundreds of years old and stand like fields* *of people with their arms open. The bulls are black as tar* *and fight the matador's sword and red cape. The people are* *conquerors, hard and proud outside, but with music and* *laughter inside.*

"Psst, psst."

I turned towards the hissing noise.

"Ana?" A short, dark-haired man pointed at me.

"Umm...*si,*" I remembered to answer in Spanish and

held up the paper. *"Para Sierra?"* I asked, to make sure we were going to the village where my great-aunt lived.

"Sierra." He nodded, took the paper and stuffed it in his pocket, then he pointed to himself and said, "Pepe."

He didn't look like a conqueror, with the buttons of his white shirt stretched across his belly and baggy grey pants rolled over muddy boots. He pointed to the bruise around my eye that was fading to yellow and clucked his tongue.

I shrugged, remembering the walk home with my father from the boxing match, both of us with one lid puffed closed. I'd felt stupid, and sorry, and furious at my father for making me take boxing lessons. I swore that I would never take another useless lesson. He vowed that he would never waste the money on me again. Hard words. They still hurt.

The buildings of Madrid loomed over roads packed with cars rushing forward like schools of fish. I was relieved when we passed through the city traffic and drove into the hills. After driving for a while, Pepe stopped at a cluster of farm buildings. He disappeared inside and came back with an old woman and several dozen eggs in his arms. The old woman got in beside me and gave me a toothless smile. Every time Pepe overtook a car on the narrow road, she fingered a string of rosary beads and prayed under her breath.

The sun was beaming into the windows and my T-shirt stuck to my back. I drifted off to sleep. When I woke up, the old woman was gone and we had stopped at a roadside café. Pepe went in and came out with a cold bottle of orange soda and a fresh roll of bread filled with a sweet, mild cheese. We sat on the hood of the car and ate.

He pointed to grey mountains in the distance. "Sierra."

My destination seemed far away, and we'd already been driving a long time. Pepe made several more stops along the way, while I slumped down on the hot plastic seat and drifted in and out of sleep.

I awoke with a start to the sound of a loud horn. I sat up and saw we were skimming past the walls of the houses that lined a very narrow street. This didn't seem to bother Pepe, who roared through the village at top speed. The final incline was so steep I thought the car would topple backwards, but we shot over the crest of a hill and entered a square lined with old buildings. It was late afternoon and the sun was still blazing down from high in the sky. Was it stuck there? The street was empty, the balconies deserted, their doors shuttered against the heat. It was like a ghost town from another century. I peeled my back away from the hot seat and stepped out of the car.

"Psst, psst." Pepe brought my attention to a door behind me that was high enough to let a horse and carriage through. Cut into it was a smaller doorway with a bronze knocker in the shape of a woman's hand. Pepe brought it down sharply a few times. The sound flew around the empty square. A stout woman with soft, brown hair streaked with silver, and a warm smile, opened the door. She wore a flour-streaked apron over a dress printed with bright sunflowers. We stepped into a dim entrance where the smell of cooking was heavy in the air. The strangeness of the place made my stomach ache. She took my suitcase and paid Pepe, I think well, because he smiled and patted me on the head before he left.

I followed her through another door which led, surprisingly, to a courtyard shaded with palm trees. There I saw flowering bushes and hanging baskets filled with pink and red geraniums. The floors and walls were covered in mosaic tiles that made dazzling geometric patterns. A peacock paraded slowly by, his tail feathers dragging on the floor.

We crossed the courtyard and entered a cool, unlit passageway. I was expecting to go upstairs, remembering the towering façade of the house, but instead we travelled down stone steps that looked as if they'd been cut out of a rock bed. The further down we walked, the cooler it grew. At the bottom, we travelled along a passageway and came to a room with tall windows open to a view of terraced hills and farm fields. The room was decorated with tapestries and sturdy, dark furniture.

We passed through to a smaller sitting room. From the door, the winged backs of two beige armchairs looked like moths ready to fly into the enormous stone mouth of the fireplace. This room seemed empty, but my guide said something in a language I didn't recognize.

"English, please, Amalia. We have nothing to hide from the child," a brittle voice answered her.

"Go to her." Amalia pushed me towards one of the chairs.

I stepped in front of the chair and jumped back, almost falling into the fireplace. The old woman in front of me looked like a creature from a Sinbad movie, with one eye that took up half her face, its pupil pulsing in response to the play of light on the wall. She moved the magnifying lens clipped to her glasses to the side, and her eye returned to a normal size. "Hello," the woman said.

She was much older than I'd thought she would be. Her face and hands were lined with fine creases and her grey hair was cut above her shoulders and stood askew in an open challenge to comb or brush.

"Hello." My response was more of a breath than a word.

"Dawdled along the way, didn't you?"

"The driver went a couple of –"

"Yes, we know what Pepe is like." She waved my explanation away. "Had trouble finding your foot, did you?"

"...pardon?"

"To put it down." She smiled at her own joke. I must have been staring, slack-jawed, because she continued brightly. "I am glad you're here." She clasped my hands and studied me. "You look like your grandmother. It's been a long time since I saw her. Welcome, welcome."

"Thanks." I held out a letter. "My mother wrote you."

She took the letter and placed it on a tray in front of her, shifting a cloth that lay covering something, and I caught the glitter of a gem. I was too tired to strike up a conversation and wanted to be alone after the long trip and the strangeness of the new place. She seemed to sense this.

"Are you tired, Ana?" I nodded. "Then Amalia will show you to your room. We'll talk after you've rested. Dinner is at nine o'clock."

Amalia led me to a small room, dark except for a beam of light that came in through a stone shaft in the wall. It seemed as if it had been built into the side of the cliff. I looked down the shaft and thought of crawling into it to see what was at the base, but the thought of slipping out and falling to an unknown distance below made me step back from the wall. How I had let myself be sent here? I hadn't wanted to spend the whole summer with someone I didn't know, even if she was my great-aunt who had long ago come to Spain from Canada. My parents always told me to stand up for myself, but they became very stern whenever I did. Everybody talked about standing up for yourself, I decided, but nobody seemed to like it when you did.

Amalia was closing the door, and the light in the room faded almost to black. I stopped her in a panic. "Can you leave the door open?"

She hesitated. "The wind comes through the tunnels and will slam it. Here is the electric light." She flicked on a bright candelabra of small light bulbs and left.

I sat on the bed. What a strange place. I looked through the narrow opening in the wall. I was high up, on a ledge or a cliff; I could tell by the hills below. The room reminded me of a cave – or a dungeon – with its stone walls and floor. It was plainly furnished with a dark, heavy table and chair, and the narrow, high bed I sat on. There was a chest of drawers for my clothes and books, but no closet to hang anything in. The wind outside started to moan in a way that sounded like human voices, and I could hear creaking in the hallway outside my room. I peeked out. The light was off, and tunnels of darkness extended in all directions. I closed the door quickly, propped the chair against it, and curled up on the bed. I was a prisoner until someone turned on the lights in the hall.

TWO

I SLEPT THROUGH DINNER INTO THE EARLY MORNING hours of the next day. My room was cold and the shaft in the cliff glowed with weak light. I slipped into my clothes and peeked out the door again. There were pools of light along the corridor from wall lamps that had been turned on. Relieved, I hurried down the hall and found my way into the kitchen, a warm room with two wide, wooden tables, copper pans suspended from a rack, and sacks of flour and sugar on the counter.

Amalia was making herself coffee. She poured me a glass of hot, sweet milk, darkened with a bit of coffee. I was hungry, and it was delicious.

"What time is it?" I asked. My watch said one o'clock.

"Seven." She smiled at my sleepy confusion. "Come. Today you help me make churros, and I will give you a fantastic breakfast." She grabbed one side of a basket filled with supplies and cooking utensils and pointed for me to grab the other side.

Outside, the square was transformed. Shuttered balcony doors were thrown open to the morning air, the owner of the kiosk that sold newspapers and candy was putting out magazine racks, and a few dogs were sniffing under café tables for leftovers from the night before.

I could smell coffee as we passed the open door of the café, before stopping at a stall on the patio beside the café tables. Amalia unlocked the door and propped open a wooden board over a window. Inside was a stove and a stool by a narrow counter where people placed their orders. Amalia lit a propane burner and started heating a huge pot of oil. She made dough from boiling water and flour. I helped her beat it together, until we were both splattered with flecks of dough.

"Bravo," Amalia said when I dropped the spoon. She finished off the work neatly, then fed the dough into a tube.

Our first visitor was the café owner, Antonio, a short, older man, about the same age as Amalia, with a handsome, deeply tanned face and friendly eyes. He leaned into the stall to say hello, and Amalia's face lit when she saw him. She smoothed her hair and leaned forward to talk to him. It seemed like a good time to leave the crowded stall and look around outside.

There was a fountain in the centre of the square and some benches under the shade of old trees. An old man wearing a worn jacket and pants that had lost their shape brought a herd of about fifteen goats through the streets. He tapped his cane and whistled, and I admired how he guided the herd to the passage that led to the lower section of town. The moment they passed from sight I heard a car horn blaring and the frantic clattering of goat bells.

Pepe's taxi hurtled over the crest of the hill. He drove halfway around the square without slowing down and squealed to a stop as if at some invisible line. He got out of the car and rushed around to the back passenger door, opening it with his head bowed as he addressed someone inside. *"Disculpeme, Comandante,* forgive me, the delay was unavoidable."

An old man stepped out and scowled at Pepe. His eyes were so black it looked like they were all pupil. He had no lips, and it seemed, horribly, that his skin curled into his mouth. I felt a chill crawl up my back. Pepe waited humbly for his fare. The man didn't look at him and walked stiffly through his door, closing it with a firm tug. He hadn't paid!

Pepe waited a while longer. He looked at the kiosk owner, who had stopped putting out newspapers to watch, and the two shrugged their shoulders. Pepe got

back in his car, sat thinking for a moment, then shrugged again and drove off. I looked up at the house. The man was at the window, looking down at me. Even from a distance, I could feel how cold his eyes were. I turned and went back into the stall. I had an uneasy feeling about this man. Why didn't Pepe try to argue or call the police? He'd seemed afraid. Maybe the man was a bully. It made me think of Marky. I wouldn't give him any more taxi rides if I were Pepe.

A few customers were standing outside the window of the stall when I returned, and Amalia greeted me with a happy cry. She lifted a coil of golden fried dough out onto a paper towel, sprinkled it with sugar, and showed me how to thread a stiff string through the coils and tie it in a circle so people could carry it next door to the café, where they ordered hot chocolate to go with their churros.

It was busy, and we spent the next hour serving a crowd of people who asked my name and stared at me with curiosity while they waited for their orders. When it slowed down, Amalia filled the pot with a fresh coil of dough and sent me to Antonio's for two hot chocolates, which he made dark and thick.

When I got back to the stall, Amalia had a heap of churros ready. "Take these home."

My great-aunt was waiting for me. "Choose your

chair, my dear. There are a number of them along this wall where you get the view." She lifted her hand towards a line of shuttered doors that had been thrown open.

I put the tray down on a small table and sank into the nearest chair, covered in worn velvet. The view was beautiful. Mist curled up from the valley, and the sun threw its rays across the sky, bringing the hills from deep blue to the colour of golden sand.

"Let's have the goodies." She rubbed her hands together.

I dipped a *churro* into my hot chocolate and bit into it. I couldn't help sighing with pleasure. It was crisp on the outside, chewy on the inside, and delicious with the hot chocolate.

"One of Amalia's specialties. You'll find she's an excellent cook. Did you sleep well?" she asked.

"Yes." I didn't tell her I had kept the light on and barricaded the door with a chair. "Doesn't anyone use the upstairs part of the house?" I asked wistfully.

"I use it in the winter. But in the summer it's too hot. This section built into the cliff is cool and comfortable."

"It's dark," I noted.

"Yes, these rooms were originally part of a series of caves connected by tunnels. They would have hidden fugitives during the time of the Inquisition, when the Jews and Moors were driven out of Spain."

I sat up. "You mean people were hiding down here?"

"Yes, around five hundred years ago," she said.

The rooms were in good shape for being five hundred years old, I thought. The walls in the sitting room had been whitewashed and were bright and smooth.

Eleanor continued. "Many people have used and improved the tunnels over time. This house was built when Napoleon was in Spain. The stairway down to the tunnels was probably finished then. In times of war and revolution, many people built their homes with a back way out. In fact, this place has a whole labyrinth of tunnels, some that connect to other houses along the square." She smiled when she saw my eyebrows lift in surprise. "Most of those passages have been sealed," she added. "Anyway, explore at will. We want you to feel at home."

The tunnel system, which I was really curious about, was too dark for me to venture through, so in the afternoon I set out to look around upstairs. The first door I opened led into a hot, dusty room that smelled like it had been sealed up for a long time. Light leaked in from between the slats of the closed blinds, filling the room with dim light. I pulled up the blinds and pushed open the doors to a small balcony, letting a waft of air in. There were books stacked on shelves that reached to the ceiling, and in the middle of the room was a large writing desk covered with piles of paper, as if someone had left in the middle of working on something. The shelves behind the desk were also filled with papers. I pulled a file towards me. The outside cover had an old photograph taped to it of a smiling, chubby boy, and underneath was written, LUIS. Who was Luis? I looked inside and found a letter.

October 6, 1937

Mama,
I started a letter to you twice before. The first time it was ruined in the rain and the second time I think someone used it to light a fire. It's very cold and we only have one blanket each. We sleep outside, but since it has been raining so much we made ourselves a tent.

I sat down in the chair and turned the page. The writing was in simple Spanish and I could follow it easily.

I met a friend here. I'm so lucky to be with him. His nickname is Flaco because he's skinny. I think his bones are growing faster than his skin and they stick out in knobs everywhere. He's only a year younger than me. A little brother. Fifteen years old. He told me he joined because he was hungry. The food is good, but not enough since all we do is sit around, which makes us think about food even more. We made friends with the cook and sometimes he gives us bread or beans between meals.

I've been waiting for my leave for months, thinking I would come and see you in the hospital, but this morning they told us that all leaves are cancelled. After the news, we were disappointed and then they sent us to do a bad job. There was fighting all night. We were moved closer to the line and I couldn't sleep with all the noise. In the morning, we were ordered into a village to look for men who were hiding. The captain stood in the middle of the street with a megaphone shouting, "It's no use hiding, we will find you. Come out and give yourselves up. The consequences will be worse if we have to come after you."

Where was this boy writing from? It seemed as if he was in an army. But would a fifteen-year-old and a sixteen-year-old be soldiers? And what was the war?

Flaco and I were sent to start at the bottom of the street. It felt bad to go into people's homes. They looked at us like we were monsters, coming into their homes with our muddy boots and our rifles. Everyone was cooking and the smell drove me crazy. Flaco asked for some soup and they gave it to us. In the end, we just went in and asked for soup at every house. We could hear the captain screaming threats through the megaphone in the street. In the last house, a man panicked. Flaco knocked on the wall to show that everything was fine and we were leaving and the man fell out of a cupboard on his knees, begging for mercy. We waited while his wife packed his suitcase and helped him into his coat.

Outside it was crazy. The other teams were throwing men out in the street without their shoes and shirts on. They were dragged through the mud to the truck and pushed inside. Flaco helped carry the man's suitcase, and we gave him a hand into the truck. He held his suitcase on his lap and looked out at his wife and children. When we turned around, the captain had stopped shouting and was staring at us.

Why were they going into people's homes and taking prisoners? This wasn't how wars were fought. I thought of the illustrations in my history books of lines of soldiers pointing rifles. This wasn't soldiers against soldiers. This was people cooking and doing everyday normal things being arrested.

Now Flaco and I have been separated. The captain said we were as dumb as a bag of sticks and then he spent the rest of the day yelling at us and asking if we wanted to make hotel reservations for our prisoners.

I am miserable. It is raining again. I hear the dinner bell, but it sounds like it's under water. I will write tomorrow. Give my love to Consuelo. Stay well, Mama. I can't wait to see you,

Luis

Consuelo! That was Abuela's name. How did this boy know my grandmother? I went over the letter again, looking for clues, but the only thing I found was a question scribbled in the margins: "What did the Guardia Civil do to Luis?"

Amalia appeared at the door. "Come, she is waiting for you."

"But...." I looked at the papers.

"Another day." She smiled at me, and I reluctantly left the desk.

THREE

M Y GREAT-AUNT WAS WAITING FOR ME IN THE courtyard. "Are those your walking shoes?" she asked, pointing with her walking stick at the canvas running shoes that I'd doodled all over with a blue pen.

"Well, yeah, I walk in these," I grinned.

"Hmmph!" She managed to put a lot of scorn into one sound. "Come along then, we're going to the hills."

We set out in the direction of the house where the man lived who had left Pepe's taxi without paying. I looked up at the window in the second storey. The white curtains were closed. This was one person I didn't want to visit, and I was relieved when we passed his front door and entered a passageway beside his house. It was dark from the shade of high walls and only wide enough for one person to walk through at a time. My great-aunt went first, walking slowly with her cane, and as I followed her, I had the feeling that someone was creeping up behind me. I turned around to see if anyone was there, but all was clear and silent at my back.

"Who lives in that house?" I asked.

"Carlos Montilla."

"I saw him leave Pepe's taxi without paying."

"Yes, he thinks he has special privileges."

"Special privileges?"

"Montilla's a retired police officer. He thinks he's above the law. Stay away from him," she warned. So that was why Pepe hadn't made a fuss.

We came out to a footpath that was flat and led through a meadow at the top of the cliff. Our shoes crushed wild thyme as we walked, and the air was filled with its perfume.

"This is as far as I go," my great-aunt said after we'd arrived at a lookout point. "Let's sit." She settled herself, then turned and looked at the mountains in the distance.

"Umm...Great-Aunt Eleanor?"

"Don't call me that."

"Oh? What should I call you?"

She was thoughtful as she looked at me. "This is the first time in twenty-four hours that you're addressing me by name. The name used to have a place in conversation. It was a way to show respect, to acknowledge that the person was important enough to remember, do you understand, Miss Ana Reid?"

I nodded, embarrassed.

"Whom do I have the pleasure of addressing? was what I was taught to ask," she continued.

"Do you expect me to talk like that?" I couldn't hide my disbelief.

She threw her head back and laughed. I was so relieved, I rolled on the ground, laughing with her.

"Call me Eleanor," she said, smiling. "That great-aunt business is long-winded and stuffy. Besides, I don't like titles, even family ones."

"Okay." I lay back and caught my breath.

As I watched the cloudless sky, I thought of the question on the bottom of Luis's letter: *What did the Guardia Civil do to Luis?* "Who is the *Guardia Civil?*"

"They are the civil guard, Spain's national police. Sort of like the Mounties are in Canada."

"So they're good guys?"

She looked amused. "That would be an oversimplification. The *Guardia Civil* have been both good and bad depending on the time in history."

"When were they bad?"

She looked at me. "Your grandmother didn't tell you?" I shook my head. "There was a terrible war among the people of Spain. An army general named Franco led an attack against the government of Spain and the people who'd elected it. At the risk of putting this too simply, I suppose I could say it was a fight between the rich and the poor, between the people who had land and power and those who had nothing. After three years of fighting, Franco won, and afterwards he sent the *Guardia Civil* around to clean house – to find anyone who was against him. They were very cruel."

"So Luis fought in the army?" I wondered aloud.

"Have you been looking through my papers?"

The word "no" was poised on my lips, but before I could say anything, she continued. "Of course you have. And I don't care either. I've abandoned all that. I used to sit there for hours going over every shred of paper, searching for a clue that I might have overlooked. But I haven't touched it, not for at least a year." She was flushed, and didn't look like she didn't care.

"Why can't you find him?"

"The trail is cold. I've written hundreds of letters, and as time passes, responses have shrunk to one line: *No record of Luis Garcia exists in our files.*"

I sat up. "So he's a Garcia!"

She studied me. "Your grandmother hasn't told you a thing, has she?"

I shook my head, but I was thinking of what Abuela had said. *I've lost something very special.*

"I won't pretend that doesn't surprise me," she reflected. "Sometimes people don't talk about things from the past that are painful. Luis is your grandmother's youngest brother. She had an older brother too, Alfonso, whom I married."

"How did you meet?"

"I was a nurse when I met Alfonso. My parents had put me through nursing school during the depression – though how they did it, I don't know. There was a brilliant doctor in Montreal named Norman Bethune. He believed in medical care for everyone, even the poor who couldn't afford doctors and –"

"Was he Alfonso's friend?"

"Pardon me?"

I shrugged impatiently. "What does he have to do with Alfonso?"

She sighed. "I suppose you want the short version?"

I nodded and couldn't help smiling. She was easy to talk to.

She continued. "Well, in a nutshell, the brilliant Dr. Bethune – believing in equal rights for all – went to Spain and became the head of the Canadian Medical Unit in Madrid to help the people's war effort. Inspired by him, I decided to go there too. My parents begged me to stay home for Christmas, so I left in January, 1937.

"We set up a blood transfusion service and held blood

donor clinics. We rigged up a van with refrigeration and drove through the bombed-out streets, delivering blood to hospitals and to the front lines. It had never been done before. We had the hardest time keeping the blood from going bad before we could get it to the wounded. And then, of course, we didn't know that different people had different blood types. That was discovered very soon after." She sighed. "Anyway, I thought it was the worthiest cause in the world.

"I met Alfonso one night when the city was under heavy bombing. He brought in a wounded man and he was determined he wasn't going to die. He stayed by the man's side, not letting him slip into unconsciousness.

"Then he came back often to visit the men and speak with them." She paused in a dreamy silence. There was a brightness in her face that made me see her as a young nurse, with a mess of hair spilling out of her cap, and intelligent, beautiful eyes. How could my great-uncle not have noticed her?

As if the memory was too sweet to bear, she brought her cane up and held her free hand out to me. "Give me a hand."

I got up reluctantly and pulled her up.

"It's nice to sit in the grass, isn't it? I haven't done it for years."

"Is that it?" I asked.

"You asked for the short version," she said over her shoulder as she hobbled away.

"DO YOU PLAY ANY GAMES?" Eleanor asked on the way back.

I thought of the hiding game, but that was only for Abuela. "I play chess."

Eleanor brightened. "Wonderful! We'll set up a board."

It was a relief to be inside where it was cool. Eleanor started the chess game with bishop's mate, a basic attack. I saw her coming and blocked the manoeuvre. "Oh, so you're at that level, are you?" she muttered.

Everyone has their way with chess. Señor Julio used to address his troops like a cultivated general: *Dawn has arrived, the attack is launched against the black battalions, and* (he would move a piece) *I challenge your noble bishop to a duel to the death.* Eleanor was much more of a fencer, jabbing and thrusting: *Take that! Ouch, you rascal!* I promised myself I would be calm and collected like Señor Julio, but when I lost my first piece, I fell off my chair in protest.

In four moves, Eleanor had managed to threaten my rook and, in another area of the board, she was a move away from getting my queen. I was in trouble! I had to decide which to save. My queen was more valuable, but

my rook was protecting my king. Eleanor looked like a pleased cat as she watched me sighing over my choices.

"That's how it started, you know," she said, looking over the board with me.

"What?"

"The civil war. Franco and other generals took over army garrisons in cities all over Spain."

I looked at what she had done, and realized that a pocket had been cut in my side of the board. "How?" I asked.

"It happened before people knew it. His troops managed to get control of enough cities to divide Spain."

It would be strange, I thought, to be sleeping in bed, while down the street people fought to take over the country. I couldn't imagine that happening in Canada. Or even in modern times. "When was that?"

"July 17th and 18th, 1936. It flared up in a flash."

"Well, let me see if I can win this war," I said, imagining the two armies.

"Think about your move well. Your army fought against one that was well equipped. You didn't have much in the way of weapons or soldiers, you know."

"What did I have then?"

"Spirit, courage, and ideals."

"That's not a fair fight!" I protested. I wanted the planes and tanks and soldiers.

Amalia came in and told us that lunch was ready, and we left the chess set as it was: Spain in July, 1936, at the start of the civil war.

IN MY ROOM, I saw the stack of blank postcards my mother had given me.

"Write us, please, even if it's only a word or two."

I sat down and filled one out.

Hi Mom and Dad,
I think I know why Abuela sent me here. She lost her brother, Luis, when he was 16 years old! I can't believe it! He was a soldier – poor guy. No clues yet, but I have this gut feeling about it – I mean a person can't disappear without a trace, right? Love the churros. Hate my room – it's a stone cave, dark and gloomy – but Eleanor's okay, so I think I'll survive. Write me soon, I miss you.

Love, Ana
xoxo

FOUR

"AS YOU KNOW FROM YOUR JOURNEY HERE, WE'RE ISOLATED. The first thing we'll need to arrange for you is transportation," Eleanor told me.

I prayed she wasn't thinking of Pepe.

"Yesterday Amalia scoured the village for something suitable for you. I gathered it was a bit of a problem, but Antonio came to the rescue, as of course he would – *for her.*" This seemed to annoy her.

"I probably won't do much riding around," I said, thinking of the steep roads and the heat.

"Hurry and finish. We want to start your lesson before it gets too hot." She drained her cup and stood up, leaning on her cane.

I stuffed the last crust of toast in my mouth and pushed away from the table. Amalia left the dishes and came upstairs with us. I wanted to tell Eleanor that I already knew how to ride a bicycle, but seeing her efforts to come up the stairs, I thought maybe I should pretend that I didn't. Perhaps she wanted to teach me. The idea seemed ridiculous, and my stomach did a nervous flip.

We crossed the courtyard and stepped outside. Antonio had closed his café and he stood in the centre of a group of children. A row of old men sat on the benches beside the fountain, and the kiosk owner was leaning out over his counter. Everyone was looking at me as if I was about to give a show.

"Muy buenos," Antonio inclined his head respectfully towards Eleanor, then smiled at me. *"Lista?"*

"Ready?" Amalia repeated with her light accent, which I'd learned was Flemish.

I shrugged. Antonio shooed the children away, and as they parted I saw an old motorbike leaning against a kick-stand, all rusted and dusty. I looked at it in disbelief, while Eleanor walked over and poked her cane here and there, snapping questions at Antonio.

She came back to me. "Well, Ana, we'll have to make do with it for now. It has a 49cc engine and shoddy suspension, but hopefully it'll hold together over these mountain roads. Come saddle up."

My mouth was dry. I was standing in my worst night-mare: learning something I was afraid of doing, and even worse, doing it in front of an audience where my failures would be on public display.

Sometimes when I was having a really bad dream, if I twisted back and forth, I woke up. I snapped my head back and forth quickly.

"What are you doing?" Eleanor asked.

"I'm...getting ready."

"There's no need to prepare. We'll give you all the instruction you need."

All the instruction in the world wasn't going to help me. It was like someone saying, "I'll tell you how to juggle these sharp knives. Go ahead, start throwing them in the air."

Antonio was tapping the torn plastic seat as if he was trying to get a dog to jump on a sofa. I straddled the motorbike and leaned forward to grasp the low handlebars. Antonio unfolded a pedal and told me to push it down. I pushed and the engine gave a lazy cough. The people around me shook their heads. I did it again and the engine sputtered.

"Listen, dear," Eleanor's voice sailed over the crowd. "Give it gas by turning the right handgrip while you're starting the engine – that's your accelerator there, your throttle, the equivalent of a gas pedal."

I tried again and again, jumping on the pedal and giving gas with a flick of my hand, but the bike wouldn't start. A scrawny boy kept tapping my arm and showing me how he would do it. My face felt hot and my hands were sweating. "I'm only thirteen. I can't legally drive," I pointed out.

"Nonsense. It's only a 49cc – it's like driving a kitchen appliance," Eleanor scoffed. "You've probably flooded the engine. Get off and Antonio will start it for you. Let's get on with the rest of the lesson." She seemed to be enjoying herself, acting very down-to-business. I had the impression that this was an unexpectedly heady experience for her.

Antonio straddled the motorbike, kicked the starter pedal sharply once, and revved the engine to life. The crowd clapped and cheered. I got on the bike again and Eleanor came up beside me.

"Listen carefully, Ana. Your motorbike has four gears. Here's the gear shaft by your right foot. Pull in the clutch with your left hand, then put your foot under the shaft and click it up. That's first gear. To change to second, you'll pull in the clutch and click down once; to go to third, clutch and press down again; and the same to go to fourth."

My head was swimming. "How do I know when to change?" I shouted above the loud encouragement from the villagers crowded around me.

"When the engine tells you." She shouted back. I

looked blank. "Never mind, just start up and Antonio will run beside you and tell you when to change."

"What if I go too fast for him?"

"Don't worry, dear, we won't abandon you!"

And they didn't. They pushed the bike along while I let out the clutch and followed me as I wobbled in first gear. Antonio stayed beside me, shouting, *"Segunda! Segunda!"* The crowd took up the cry, running behind me until I lost control and a net of arms caught me.

"Now, Ana, let's put together everything you've learned." Eleanor's voice parted the crowd.

"I'm tired."

"Nonsense. We've only been out here for forty-five minutes. By lunchtime you'll be riding that contraption. *Otra vez?*" she was already speaking to Antonio, getting the crowd away so I could make another pass. She turned back to me. "You need this to live here, and there is no reason why you can't do it. Engage the clutch, put the bike into first gear. Release the clutch smoothly while giving gas, and you'll be off. No namby-pambying around, no feeble tries."

There was no getting out of this. I did as she said, but no one had warned me what a flood of gas in first gear would make the motorbike do. The front wheel lifted off the ground and I sailed across the square, parting the villagers as I went, knocking down a magazine rack outside the kiosk, collecting newspapers, which flapped around me. I was heading towards the steep hill leading out of the square when the front wheel crashed down. I pulled in the clutch and clicked down with my right foot and the bike lurched forward in second gear. I was well into the mouth of the steep road when I realized that I didn't know where the brakes were. I screamed and jammed my feet against the ground, but it was too late. I could feel gravity pull me forward as the wheels abandoned themselves to the hill.

A weight hurtled onto the seat behind me and hands grasped the handlebars, pinching my fingers. We careened down the hill, heading straight for the side of a house where the road divided. I pulled the handlebars to the right. The person behind me pulled to the left. We were locked in what seemed like a long struggle for control of the steering, though we had only a second, both yelling at the top of our lungs. At the last moment, I yanked the handlebars free. We scraped against the wall and plunged down another hill, steeper even than the first one. My hands were crushed as the person behind me gripped the handlebars with all his might. I screamed.

Down we tore, past doorways filled with disbelieving faces, descending in a vertical drop along a road that looked like a waterfall of stones and ended in a dirt path that skirted the stream. The bike took on a life of its own, bouncing along the rough road. The wheels snagged in a rut, and we lifted off the seat and sailed headfirst over the bank of the stream.

My face slapped against the surface and I sank in deep, muddy water. I started crying as I came up, and when I turned around, I saw a boy my age standing in water up to his neck. He looked away from me. Antonio crouched on the bank, out of breath from running. I was lifted out of the water and the boy climbed out himself. A group of villagers had the bike upright and were inspecting it. Antonio yelled at the boy and shooed him away. He shot me a dark look before he left, and I felt bad. I had panicked and almost killed us both, and now he was being blamed. I wiped my face and squinted up at Antonio.

"Mira, Antonio...." I started, wanting to explain that it wasn't his fault. But my mouth fell open and I forgot all about it when I saw Antonio holding the bike out to me. I had almost broken my neck, my face throbbed from slapping the water, I was soaking wet, and he actually thought I was going to get on that contraption again?

I shook my head. He started the motorbike and held it out to me. I wanted to walk away, but the group of onlookers clapped and patted my back and patted the seat of the motorbike. Every time I shook my head, I was nudged towards the bike. The scrawny boy was the most enthusiastic, bouncing around and flicking his legs out. He tried to get on the bike and fell off. I couldn't help laughing. Once I laughed, everyone took it to mean that everything was okay and we were going to go on.

We were on flat open road, but the ruts were hard to steer across. We went back and forth, and as lunchtime approached, the crowd left. Even the little boy who I called Cricket lost interest and went to look for frogs in the stream. I tried to tell Antonio that it was hopeless, but he wouldn't listen. The sun climbed in the sky and the leaves hung flat in the heat. The road was bleached white. My eyes watered and I could barely keep them open in the strong light.

And then I don't know how it happened. A hundred tries were the same, and then on the next one, I did it. I did everything right. I didn't get flustered when I had to change gears, I remembered to slow down over the ruts, I steered, I braked, I gave the right amount of gas. I did everything, and felt the breeze rush past me as I sped along, whooping at the top of my lungs.

On the way home, Antonio sat behind me, and I rode into the square like a hero. Amalia was waiting for us with the big doors open. I drove straight through into the inner courtyard, making the peacock scramble away so clumsily that I laughed aloud.

I ran downstairs and found Eleanor sitting by the window

with a pair of binoculars around her neck. "Congratulations!" She looked amused. "Persistence pays off."

"Persistence is another word for torture," I mumbled, but had to admit, "it's way better than riding a bicycle."

"Good work." She got up slowly and shuffled out of the room. "I'm going for my nap – the heat in the afternoon can get unbearable. I suggest a siesta for you as well."

I wrinkled my nose. Afternoon naps were for babies.

"You can entertain yourself then?" she asked dryly.

"Sure."

I fell on the lunch plate Amalia had set aside for me. When I finished, I went up to the library to look for more letters from Luis. I couldn't bear the heat in the room, so I collected a file that said *Guardia Civil* and took it downstairs to my gloomy cave. I had to admit it was pleasantly cool.

What did the Civil Guard do to Luis? That had been the question on the letter. There had to be some clues in the file. I sat cross-legged on the bed and spread the papers out around me. There were lists of people who had been interrogated or imprisoned after the war by the Civil Guard. I didn't find Luis's name, but I did find his friend, Flaco. The entry said: *Flaco Cruz, fifteen years old, brought in for questioning, date of release unknown. He might have been held for months.* But why? He was just a hungry boy in the army. The friends had been separated somehow. Luis had disappeared and Flaco had ended up a prisoner of the Civil Guard. When was that?

I didn't get to find out because, before I knew it, my head slumped down on the papers and I was asleep.

ELEANOR LOOKED AT MY GROGGY FACE with amusement when I came into the kitchen an hour later.

"Decided to give the siesta a try," I said, wishing my cheeks weren't creased with lines from the paper I'd slept on.

Amalia smiled and put a cup of sweet, milky coffee in front of me, and some *mantecados,* lard cakes.

"I'm not really hungry." The heat had taken away my appetite.

"Come. You'll need your energy for school," Eleanor said brightly.

I paused, cup midway to my mouth. "School?"

"You're going to summer school," she said.

"What!?"

"To polish your Spanish," she explained. And when the shock stayed on my face, she added, "Oh come on, you don't want to go around sounding like you come from the last century, do you?"

"What do you mean?"

"You speak a positively archaic Spanish. You sound like you're eighty years old."

I blushed as I thought of Señor Julio, Señora Carol,

and Abuela: *My, the breath of spring is sweeter than honey and consoles my sorrow when we are apart.* They recited poems in rounds and sometimes sang their old *zarzuelas: Pretty girl of Madrid, light of verbena, you are like a sprig of lavender.* This was the Spanish I grew up listening to. No wonder people had chuckled at the churros stand when they'd been introduced to me. *Enchanted to meet you, my good neighbour.*

"It's four short weeks, mornings only. It'll be good for you. Give you something to do anyway," Eleanor said gently, noticing my embarrassment. "At least you don't have to worry about being held back a year, like the other kids. Poor ducklings." She shook her head, then seemed to realize that she wasn't making it sound very appealing, and added brightly, "It'll be fun!"

I wanted to protest that I had plenty to do. I needed to find Luis. I needed to know what happened to Flaco.

But Eleanor's mind was made up, and after our coffee, Amalia and I went across the square to Antonio's café where he was waiting for us. He drove down into the valley and showed me the way to the school, which lay on the outskirts of a village a few kilometres away. It was an easy route to remember. Then on the way home, we drove up a steep road that wound along the higher part of the hills. The sun was setting, and as I watched the golden countryside, I decided that this was the route I would take on my motorbike.

FIVE

THE NEXT MORNING, I WAS COLD WHEN I WOKE UP. I pulled the blankets around me and went to the shaft in the wall. The sky was grey, and clouds hid the hills in the distance. Amalia gave me a new plastic pencil case and a snack. I felt like I was going to kindergarten. The streets were wet when I drove out. A child with a wide black umbrella skipped in front of me. I honked my horn and a familiar face peered around at me.

"Let me pass, Cricket," I called.

He started to zigzag in front of me, giggling in a high voice that rolled down the misty street.

"Cricket!" I shouted, and finally managed to get around him. He tried to chase me, but his umbrella turned inside out and I left him behind, jumping up and down in the centre of the road, yelling after me.

On the mountain path, I stopped to watch the incredible activity of the clouds as they tumbled down hillsides and stretched into a mist around me. I thought about spending the day in the hills while I puttered slowly along, but decided not to when a fine rain started to fall.

The school building was hot, even though it was raining outside. I presented myself in the office to a man who didn't hide his annoyance at my late arrival. He led me past empty classrooms, and as we approached the end of the hall, I could hear a teacher yelling above the roar of voices.

I stood in the door, dripping wet, the smell of chalk and plastic surrounding me. There were about a dozen students of all ages in the room, even a couple of boys who looked a lot older – like they were shaving. One of them had forced a younger boy into an unwilling ball with his head stuck through his legs, and he was slapping him back and forth across the face, ignoring the teacher's shouts. He released the boy when he saw the man and me standing in the doorway. His victim's face was red and puffed from the pressure it had endured. I was surprised to recognize the boy who had fallen into the river with me. He didn't notice me, intent as he was on the retreating back of his tormentor. As soon as his tormentor was a safe distance away, he shouted an insult that I didn't understand. Judging by the reaction in the classroom, it was a daring thing to say. The older student walked straight out of the room without turning around.

"Silencio!" The man's voice silenced everybody.

After he left, there was much cheering for the younger boy, who seemed pleased with himself. The teacher told me to sit in the seat beside him and had us introduce ourselves. His name was Paco.

The older boy didn't return to class, and when I looked out the window, I saw him sweeping the playground. Later he came into the room and emptied the garbage into a large bag that he dragged behind him. Paco watched him glumly.

The morning passed slowly. The teacher gave me word lists to study for a dictation, and then we had to stand in turn and read a paragraph aloud from a story book.

Paco ran outside just as the teacher started collecting the books at the end of the class. She yelled at him to come back, but he ignored her, and I watched him hurry down the driveway to the road. A moment later, the older boy jumped on a motorbike and took off after him. I muttered, "Oh, oh."

A girl beside me shrugged, *"Son hermanos."* They were brothers. How badly could one brother hurt another without getting in trouble?

I found out when I drove up the mountain road. There was Paco clambering up the side of a hill. He had crushed grass streaked along his arms and legs, and it looked as if two pebbles had been sewn into his bottom lip. His hair, short and brown, stuck out as if it had been pulled up in fistfuls, but his honey brown eyes had a defiant sparkle in them. In the distance, his brother's motorbike rounded a bend and disappeared.

I stopped and waited while he reached the road. When he came abreast of me I said, "Your brother's a... *scoundrel.*" I blushed as the word came out. Thank you, Señor Julio. Paco looked at me, and I didn't know why, but I finished up Señor Julio's chess declaration, "who should be summarily executed or at least banished to the far regions of the land...." There was more, but I bit my tongue, expecting Paco to start laughing.

He looked delighted. "Wow."

I pointed to the back seat. He raised an eyebrow in surprise, then smiled and climbed on. I pulled hard on the gas, and the motorbike took off sharply. He grabbed me and started whooping at the top of his lungs. The morning clouds had cleared, and the air was cool against my skin as we rode through the hills. We stopped to look in a deserted farmhouse. Paco turned over rocks and showed me a white scorpion. Then we took turns riding, going off the road through fields and along abandoned paths.

Hours later we pulled up at the house, where Amalia greeted me at the door. Paco jumped off the bike when he saw her face. I suddenly realized how late it was. My punishment was that Amalia wouldn't let me eat in the kitchen, and I had to sit at the big dining-room table by myself. I didn't like eating alone.

When I finished, I brought my dishes to the kitchen with a full speech prepared, but to my relief Amalia had softened and she put a sweet flan in front of me, asking for no more explanations or apologies.

When Eleanor woke up, she came into the kitchen for coffee. "So you made it home," she said to me.

"I'm sorry, I lost track of time."

"You'll have lots of time to explore the countryside. Just let us know next time," she scolded gently.

"I will," I promised.

Amalia poured her coffee, and Eleanor carried it out of the kitchen.

"Eleanor," I called when she was at the door, "did you ever find Flaco?"

She hesitated, then turned back. "I don't know if I want to reopen this, Ana...."

"I think Abuela wanted me to know." Why else would she have sent me here? I was growing sure that Luis was who she wanted me to find.

"Then she should have told you herself," she snapped,

and stepped through the doorway. She must have hesitated in the hallway again, because her voice drifted back into the kitchen. "In a file on the left-hand side of the desk. At the very bottom."

I found the file exactly where Eleanor said it would be. There were two letters inside. The oldest had been written in 1948. Nine years after the war. It was addressed to my great-uncle Alfonso.

My esteemed Mr. Garcia,
It is my deepest honour to receive your communication and I respond to your queries about my well-being with humble gratitude. With profound thanks to God and our great leader, Franco, I and my family find ourselves in the best of health and economic conditions.

I wish you and your brother, Luis, all the best and remit this correspondence to you with the greatest respect.

Sincerely,
Eduardo (Flaco) Cruz
At the Post Office of the village of Paloma

Strange letter. Flaco seemed to think that Luis was with Alfonso nine years after the war. What would make him think that?

The second letter was also from Flaco, but it had been sent ten years after the first one. As I compared the dates on the two letters, I noticed the handwriting was different on the second one, which said:

Dear Mr. and Mrs. Garcia,

I am Juan Cruz. My father, Flaco, sits beside me and I am writing what he tells me. We got your letter last week and since then my father has been upset. He sent you a letter ten years ago with information about Luis, but your questions make him think that the scribe in the post office didn't write down what he told him. Here are my father's words:

Your brother Luis and I spent eight months together in the army, night and day, except when we were separated for a week by our captain. We were up in the mountains by Teruel and it was spring.

I was in the army because I needed to eat, and your brother was a pacifist. Together we were useless. He looked at the clouds and read his poems. This one he said often and I remembered it:

> *I am so lucky to be here in the spring fields*
> *Where the flowers lift their pale undersides*
> > *in the wind*
> *I forget I have a rifle in my arms*

When I watch the clouds climb into white towers

For the first few months, all we did was move from one place to another. We got used to the sound of guns in the distance, and we started to think that making camp and moving our lines was all that war was.

Then we were sent up to the front line. We didn't even reach the ditches when the planes started flying over us. Half of us dropped our guns in the grass and ran for cover. The planes came around again and pounded us. Luis put his hands over his ears. I kept saying his name, but he didn't hear me, even after it was quiet.

Then things went from bad to worse. Luis got malaria. Many of us had it. There wasn't enough medicine, so the doctors gave everyone a little, but not enough to cure. Luis kept getting sicker until they took him away one night. I watched the oil lamp disappear up the mountain path as they carried him away on a stretcher. That was the last I saw of him.

After the war, I was detained for weeks by the Guardia Civil while they asked questions about you, Mr. Garcia. I would have told them everything if I had known anything. They made me suffer. I tried to remember stories that Luis told me, but I couldn't, so I made things up. In the end they let me go, but if they caught your brother, they would have done worse to him, much worse.

If you hear from Luis, tell him his good friend Flaco is waiting for him.

Yours sincerely,
Flaco Cruz

What did this mean? Flaco couldn't read and write. He must have dictated his first letter to the clerk in the post office. But why had the clerk not written down what Flaco had told him? Maybe he hadn't dared write what Flaco had said about being detained and tortured by the Civil Guard. The thought made me uneasy. What kind of place had Spain been after the civil war?

I read both letters again. The first was too flowery and said nothing. Flaco wouldn't even talk like that, I guessed. What bothered me the most was the message in the second letter. Could it be true that the Civil Guard wasn't after Luis, but Alfonso, and that both brothers had been in terrible danger?

When Eleanor woke up, we returned to our chess game and I asked her about Flaco's letters.

"What he says is true. After the war everyone who fought against Franco was in danger. Even people who didn't fight were watched, and any little complaint could put a person in trouble with the Civil Guard. It was a time when the law was lawless."

She slid her bishop on a long diagonal and took my rook. I'd already decided to sacrifice him and, instead, move a pawn to protect my queen. I hoped that the pawn guarding my queen would stop Eleanor. I looked at her army. It was strong. She had more pieces left than me. She could almost afford to lose a queen. I couldn't.

"What's happening now in the war?" I asked.

"The battle of Madrid: the fight for the capital of the country. You are holding the city, but you are under siege and the National army keeps attacking roads and cities around you to cut you off. You lose lots of men...." She glanced at the line of pieces she had taken.

I didn't like this scenario. "Aren't there international fighters?"

"Yes, lots. Americans and Canadians and Irish, British and French. They help you hold the city. I was in Madrid then," she said as an aside. "No clean water, no heat, electricity, or supplies. Even driving the ambulance was hard, because so many streets were broken up by bombs."

She was looking at my queen. The most powerful piece on the board. Her hand came up and she slid her black queen forward to take mine.

I gasped, and Señor Julio came out in my outrage: *"You rogue! For this insult on the integrity of my troops you shall pay a high price."* My pawn came in from behind and toppled her queen. I liked the weight of it in my hand. "Take that!"

She frowned.

"When are we now?" I asked anxiously, looking at the half-empty board.

"Well, with your rook and queen gone now...I'd say around the autumn of 1937. Malaga in the south has been taken, and you've lost Bilbao and Santander, almost the whole northern coast of Spain."

"That's not good." I was disappointed.

"You keep a stronghold for yourself in the east, where your government is. You surprise everyone with what you manage to do with nothing. David and Goliath. Fighting a giant with a slingshot and a stone."

Eleanor left me alone at the chessboard to plan my attack. I got up every now and then and looked at the view outside, then came back and thought some more. Amalia had to drag me to the table to eat, but by then I knew how I would crush Eleanor's army.

SIX

IT WAS SUNDAY. I WAS AWAKE EARLY AND READING Flaco's letters again when Amalia called me to help her at the churros stall. I collected the papers and hurried downstairs to help her carry the basket of supplies. While we waited for the oil to heat, Antonio hung around the back door talking to Amalia, and I sat on the stool by the counter comparing the dates of Flaco's letters with the dates that he'd been imprisoned by the Civil Guard.

Cricket came skipping up to the window. I could see only his brown eyes over the counter. "Two extra-large orders of churros."

"Where's your money, little boy?" Amalia asked from behind me.

"I have it. I need the churros first."

"Show me."

"How much do you want?" he asked, digging into his pockets.

"One hundred and fifty pesetas each. Three hundred pesetas."

He put a handful of things on the counter and counted out five stones, a broken hair clip, a few beads, and two elastic bands. "That's three hundred pesetas," he pushed the pile forward and took away a one-hundred-peseta coin, "and this is mine."

Amalia knocked her fist on the counter. "Give me the coin, little boy. And I will give you back your three hundred pesetas here."

Cricket smiled at the deal she was offering him. "For two extra-large orders?"

"Two extra-large orders will not fit in your skinny belly."

Cricket didn't like this. He held onto his coin and tapped it on the counter. "My belly has a secret door where I can put –"

"Come on, you're holding up the line!" Paco shouted, butting him aside. "I want six," he ordered.

Amalia lifted out an extra big coil of churros. I sugared it, tied it with string and dangled it in front of Cricket, and he released his coin to me.

Paco's brothers and mother were already sitting with their hot chocolates. It was a beautiful morning and the café was filling quickly. I handed out Paco's order, and when he stepped aside, came face to face with Carlos Montilla.

It was like stepping into a spray of cold mist; it shocked me, and I stared at him with my mouth open.

"One order." His voice was soft and cold.

I turned to repeat the order, but Amalia had already seen him. "Good morning, sir," she called out.

He nodded towards her and turned his gaze on me. It felt as if his eyes were floating out of their sockets towards me. "Who's this?" he asked.

"This is Ana, the señora's great-niece."

"This is the first time you've come to visit," he said, as if it was abnormal.

"My grandmother sent me."

"Your grandmother?" Was it my imagination, or did his eyes turn an even darker shade of black? "What is her name?"

"Consuelo Garcia."

His lips mouthed the name, but not a whisper came out of his mouth. His back was stiff and straight, as if it was a slab of wood. He was like a big puppet with a human mask on. He wore a powder blue sweater that was creased along the sleeve as if it had been ironed. Strange. Behind Montilla stood a polite line of customers. No one shouted out orders or talked over anyone else like they usually did.

I looked at Amalia to see if his order was ready, and when I turned back, he was still studying me.

"It must be boring for you, spending so much time in the house...."

"I go to summer school," I said.

The grocer behind Montilla, who was listening to our conversation, nodded approvingly. "On her motorcycle."

Amalia lifted the churros out, sugared them, and put them in a paper cone.

"Be careful on the mountain roads," Montilla warned me as he paid, "it's a long way down."

After he left, the line surged forward and we were busy with orders for the rest of the morning. Once it was quiet enough that Amalia didn't need me, I took a ring of churros home. In the kitchen, I reached into my pocket for the papers I'd been looking at. I would ask Eleanor to fill in some of the gaps while we ate. I checked my front pockets, then my back, and then the churros basket. The letters were gone!

I tried to remember if I had even put them away before it got busy. Who came to the counter? First Cricket, then Paco and...Montilla! Could he have seen the letters sitting on the counter? All of a sudden, I felt sick. What if he had them?

I ran back to the stall. Amalia was just about to close the back door.

"Wait! I think I lost something."

"What?"

I couldn't tell her what I'd lost. Alfonso and Eleanor had waited years to get the letters, especially the second one that told the truth, and I might have let it fall into the wrong hands. "A piece of paper."

Amalia held the door wide open and daylight filled the stall. I didn't see it anywhere. I circled the outside of the stall, but it was gone.

"Is it important?"

"No," I answered as dread flooded over me.

Time crawled by while I tried to figure out where I could have put the letters. I turned through every page of what I had carried with me, I went out to the stall and around the kiosk at least five times, until people started asking me what I was looking for and if they could help. How could I tell Eleanor that I'd lost Flaco's letters?

I didn't sleep well and was up early the next morning, looking in the library. Maybe I had left it there after all. I opened the balcony doors to let the morning air in. The square was empty, and across the street I was surprised to see Paco at Montilla's door. I stepped back into the room and watched. He knocked and waited. It took a long time for the door to be answered. Paco held out a package wrapped in plain brown paper. Montilla accepted it and closed the door without saying anything, then Paco ran back to his house. What was he delivering so early in the morning?

I could hear Amalia calling me in the courtyard. I had to eat and get ready for school. I would ask Paco about it later. His older brothers usually gave him a ride on their way to the market where the family had a butcher stall. They never stopped the truck, they just slowed down and Paco jumped off the back and landed running until he could stop.

At school we didn't talk much. Paco played soccer during recess with the rest of the boys. There were only three girls and they walked around arm in arm, speaking in a tight group. That left me by myself most of the time. I walked through the orchards or sat in the meadow by the front gate watching the blue sky. My friendship with Paco wasn't meant to be a secret, but somehow it had turned into one. It was fun to be together when we were alone, but when all of the boys were together they didn't want the company of a girl. So Paco and I ignored each other at school. I didn't like it, but we had such a good time after school that I didn't say anything. When class was over, Paco was the first one to leave, running down the road until he was out of sight. I always found him on the way home, waiting for me at the side of the road.

"I saw you this morning," I said when I caught up to him after school.

He didn't seem to care. "Let me ride," he said, grabbing the handlebars.

I put the motorbike in neutral and got off. "What were you giving Montilla?" I asked.

"Sausages."

"Oh." I was disappointed. "Why?"

He shrugged. "My grandmother sends me."

Montilla had his food delivered. This didn't tell me anything about him. He probably just got special treatment in the village.

"Let's go see that ruin over there." Paco pointed to the crumbling walls of a building that sat on the crest of a hill behind the school and turned the motorbike around.

WE CLIMBED OVER THE GARDEN WALL and cut through a tangle of plants until we reached a window without bars where we could climb into the old, abandoned building.

We stepped into a central reception room with ceilings that disappeared into darkness high above us where the light didn't reach. It felt like the darkness was going to fall down on me like a net. I crossed the foyer quickly and headed to a large, light-filled room on the other side. The floor was scattered with garbage, rusted iron bed frames, and mattress springs. Paco walked through without interest, and presently I heard a loud clanging coming from beyond the room. I found him at the end of a corridor trying to break a locked chain around a gate, with a rock. His pounding shook the walls and filled the air with drifts of dust. He gave a final tremendous blow. The chain dropped to the ground, and the gate swung ajar.

We hesitated, surprised, then Paco patted his pockets and pulled out a box of matches. He wrapped a rag around a stick and lit it. It made a smoky torch. The light showed the line where the patterned stone walls ended and a rough tunnel began. When we stepped inside, our feet sank in a layer of dust and earth. It felt as if the darkness was wrapping around my neck, and I could feel my throat tightening. My steps faltered.

Paco squeezed my hand, pulling me along. "Come on, Ana."

I took a few more steps, but my knees were growing shaky and it was getting hard to breathe. Paco kept coaxing me as the light at our backs vanished, "Don't worry, Ana. There's nothing here."

He moved ahead, and the passage grew so narrow that our shoulders stubbed against the walls. I grabbed the back of his shirt, almost tearing it. Thankfully, the passage opened up to an area where we could see walls of blue-grey stone, like waterfalls. There was a light source somewhere. Paco's face was powdery in the darkness, his eyes shaded by soft black circles. It was a welcome sight. We walked through the cave, that was high and narrow, like a fissure in the rocks, and when we turned a corner, a slit of hot white light stabbed at our eyes. We walked up to it and peered out. We were halfway up the cliff, looking out at the sun-baked fields below. There was a narrow ledge outside that led across the cliff to a stone slope.

It looked like someone had camped here. We found a rough wooden bench and the remains of a blanket half buried in the ground. Paco picked up the blanket with a stick and threw it against the wall. A piece of material in bands of red, yellow, and purple caught in a puff of air and floated down to the ground. It was a flag – but of which country? I stuffed the flag in my bag and followed Paco out the opening onto the ledge. We walked across to the stony slope and clambered up to the road. The heat pressed on my back, and I could hardly wait to get home to the coolness of my room in the cliff.

On the way back, we came upon a group of boys playing soccer in a field at the base of the village. Paco told me to stop, and when I did, he got off. A few of his friends came up, curiously looking between us. Paco talked to them and I waited, trying to look casual. Something about his back told me not to ask him if he was coming with me. I gassed the throttle to remind him I was there. The other boys looked at me, but Paco ran towards the field, calling for the ball. It was kicked to him, and he bounced it off his head, running into the game.

SEVEN

As I walked the motorbike into the courtyard, I wondered if I should give up on trying to be friends with Paco. What was wrong with him? He acted as if he was embarrassed to be with me. Maybe he was only my friend when he wanted a ride home.

I brought a few crumbs that were left over from Amalia's snack out of my school bag and scattered them around for the small, brown sparrows that flew down from under the shade of the roof. My hand squeezed the softness of the flag in my bag, and I wondered what Eleanor would have to say about it. I found her sitting in front of doors flung open to the view, watching the hills in the distance sink into clouds. A storm was coming.

She looked at me with curiosity. "Well? How are the ways of the world?"

I pulled the faded flag out of my bag and held it so

she could see the bands of red, yellow, and purple.

She looked shocked. "Where did you find this?"

"At the place over there." I pointed across the valley where the ruin was barely visible.

"The old monastery," she said. "This was the state flag of the Spanish Republic. When Franco won, the flag became yellow with a red band in the centre. I haven't seen a flag like this since the war."

"It looked like someone was hiding in a horrible cave under the monastery."

"Many people hid after the war. Anyone who fought for the Republicans was an enemy of Franco and had to be protected. You went down there by yourself?" She was surprised.

"I went with Paco." I couldn't help making a face when I said his name.

"What about him?" she asked.

"I don't know...."

"You're out with him every day," she coaxed.

"He only rides with me when no one is around, like on the way home from school."

She raised an eyebrow. "Oh?"

I chewed my lip and avoided her gaze. I didn't know why he acted the way he did, and I was sure talking about it would just make me feel depressed.

"So what do you do when someone doesn't treat you

like a friend?" Eleanor persisted.

I shrugged. "Just get over it...or make some new friends."

"No! Friendships are among the most valuable of life's relationships. You don't want one that crumbles every time it's tested." She was in a genuine huff. "Come with me," she pulled herself up. "You have something to learn from your family."

I followed her down a corridor to a room that looked like a laboratory. It was full of instruments, jars holding tweezers and cotton swabs, cans of compressed air, bottles of rubbing alcohol.

"Have a seat." She pointed to a chair and began putting things on the table while she talked: eyepieces, tweezers, alcohol, swabs, a soft cloth.

"You don't know much about your family history. It's not your grandmother's fault," she added quickly, "sometimes people don't want to talk about the past when it's caused them pain."

"She missed Spain." This was the one thing I was sure of.

"Yes, so did Alfonso. But he didn't have the choice to stay either. We had to leave quickly when Franco won the war. We travelled across the Pyrenees mountains by foot and made it to France. Then we waited for Luis."

"Where was Abuela?"

"I managed to get your grandmother to Montreal

before we left. My family was waiting for her there. It was a good thing, too. World War II started and Hitler invaded France."

"Where did you go then?"

"We were stuck there. We didn't have money, we didn't have travel documents. Every day it was harder to hide from the German police."

"Couldn't someone help you?"

"The Germans went wherever they wanted, into people's homes, into factories and restaurants. We were stopped one morning while we were walking along a country road. We didn't have papers, so they made us get on a truck carrying prisoners and took us to a concentration camp by the beach in Marseilles."

"Did you try to escape?" I couldn't imagine Eleanor taking anything lying down.

"There was no way to get out. We lived for two years on that beach. I hate sand – it's one of my pet peeves now. There was no escaping with the barbed-wire fences and guards. Besides, we were so hungry and weak we could barely walk out when they liberated us." She sat down beside me. "After the war, we ended up in Antwerp. We wanted to stay in Europe until we found Luis."

"Where's Antwerp?"

"It's in Belgium. Antwerp, as it happens, is the diamond trading centre of the world. Did you know that?"

I shook my head.

"We didn't plan on working in the diamond trade, but we fell into it. I've learned a lot over the years from looking inside stones." She pulled a lamp forward and turned it on. "You have to know how to use light when you're examining a gem." She adjusted the angle of the lamp and brought out a narrow box. Inside was a line of glittering diamonds.

"Choose a stone."

"They all look the same."

"They do, but they're as different from each other as you and I."

I looked again. The diamonds were the same size and were all cut in the same style.

"Alfonso and I used to buy diamond lots. We always got some that weren't worth selling. Let's see if you can find out why."

I pointed to a diamond in the middle of the line. It seemed to sparkle a bit more than the rest. "That one," I said.

"Pick it up with the tweezers. Now dip one of the brushes on the tray in alcohol and stroke it gently. Many flaws wash off."

I brushed the diamond carefully, admiring the soft colours of light reflecting from it.

Eleanor picked up a small magnifying glass. "This

loupe magnifies ten times. It's hard to focus at first. Bring the diamond up to the loupe slowly. Stop when it's in focus."

I tried more than once, but I couldn't get the diamond in focus.

As if she knew what I was struggling with, Eleanor said, "You won't get it all in focus. Turn and tilt the stone. Look in one facet or side at a time."

"What am I looking for?"

"Tell me what you see."

I rotated the stone slowly. "I see a bunch of scratchy lines."

"Polish lines. See if you can find some inclusions – those are internal flaws." She waited a moment in silence while I examined the diamond. "Each stone has a character," she continued. "Some are harder than others, some have rare things hidden inside."

The inside of the diamond was a well of geometric light and shapes. It was hard to make out anything but the brilliance and beauty of the stone.

"It's beautiful."

She nodded. "I've grown to appreciate them – not because of what people will pay for them, but because of how they are formed. They come through volcanic fire, and pressure over millions of years, with the greatest beauty and hardness."

"That's why robbers use them to cut open windows," I said, thinking aloud.

She chuckled.

I sat forward. "There's a ghost shape floating in here."

She nodded. "Yes, it's an internal flaw. Good, that wasn't easy to find." She looked at me. "But you already know you're good at finding things, don't you?" She continued without waiting for an answer.

"You know, sometimes in the years in Antwerp, while we were searching for Luis, I would tell myself, *Eleanor, these years are the volcanic years, and you are making of your life something strong and worthwhile.*"

This wasn't what I'd expected to hear. I'd thought I'd just get another lecture on standing up for myself and not letting my friends run my life. But as I helped Eleanor put things away, it struck me how pathetic a wishy-washy friendship was. Eleanor and Alfonso had never given up on Luis, even when it felt hopeless. They'd stayed loyal through thick and thin. I wondered how long my friends and family would look for me if I was lost.

Forever, I hoped.

THAT NIGHT I SAT ON THE BALCONY watching Montilla's house. The front looked like a fortress. Every window was covered with heavy, black bars. Even if I was foolish enough to try, there was no way to get in other than being invited through the front door. The lights were out in the front room, which meant Montilla must be at the back of the house. I went outside and bought some sunflower seeds at the kiosk, then walked around the square until I came to the passage between the houses. I was surprised to see lights fastened to the walls that made it quite bright. I looked around. It was a pleasant evening. People were sitting in the café. The world seemed friendly and safe. There was no reason why I couldn't stroll through the passage to see what was happening at the back of Montilla's house.

I walked through quickly and came out behind Montilla's house, where I saw his silhouette in the window. A lighter flared in his hand, and he ignited a piece of paper and watched it curl up before he released it into what looked like a wastebasket on his desk. The back of his house was protected by a stone wall topped with broken glass, and I couldn't get closer to look in the window. I could see fire leaping up from the container on his desk. This was not a normal thing to do. At home we put old paper in the recycling bin, we didn't light bonfires on our desks. What was he getting rid of? I thought of Flaco's letters.

Montilla picked up another page and paused. He was as still as I was. A creepy feeling started in my stomach, then exploded into my chest. Was he facing away from me or towards me? I couldn't tell from his silhouette. The light in the room went off, and he disappeared in the darkness. Now I was the one exposed in the middle of the field bathed in moonlight.

I made my way quickly back through the passageway and crossed the square to our door. I didn't stop or look back once. Watching Montilla was hard. He seemed to have a sixth sense about what was around him. Maybe it was the years of police work. He knew how to watch better than I did. And that was something I hadn't counted on.

EIGHT

I LIKED THE MORNING MIST. IT MADE THE COUNTRYSIDE look like an enchanted land from a storybook. I took my time driving along the mountain roads on my way to school. I knew where the potholes were and wove along the road avoiding them. It was a surprise when I heard the hum of a car engine behind me. Most cars used the paved road below and didn't bother with the slow, winding mountain road. I sped up a bit, and the car sped up as well. I looked over my shoulder, and there was a dark vehicle with tinted windows following close behind. I moved to the side of the road to let it pass. The car came closer, so close that it was only a few metres away.

I remembered Montilla's warning that it was a long way down from the mountain roads and checked behind my shoulder again. The car seemed to leap forward, and with a jolt, I knew I was in danger. One bump would send me over the edge. I looked ahead, trying to figure out how I could escape. I couldn't get off the road, because a low stone wall blocked me. I knew there was at least a quarter of a kilometre of the wall left before it ended at an open field I could ride into. My heart was pounding. I accelerated and put the bike in top gear, swerving around potholes and charging for the end of the stone wall. The car accelerated too, and I could hear it behind me, crashing over potholes, its fender banging against the ground.

The end of the stone wall was up ahead. I stood up on the seat, willing my bike to go faster. As soon as I reached the opening, I turned up into the field and raced across the stony ground. When I looked back over my shoulder, the car with its mysterious dark windows was driving away. Whoever the driver was could have easily run me down on the highway, but on the mountain road I'd just been able to stay ahead. My heart was still racing. The rest of the way to school I drove across fields and along footpaths where a car couldn't go.

My legs were weak when I got off my motorbike at school. Paco came across the playground. *"Que pasa?"* he asked, studying my face. What's the matter?

"I think someone in a car was trying to run me down." I could feel tears well up in my eyes as I described the car and how it had chased me.

Paco chewed on his lip and looked behind him at a group of his friends who were watching us and waiting for him. "It was just someone in a hurry," he said, backing away.

"No, it wasn't!"

He was already standing with his friends. "Whatever," he shrugged his shoulders.

It struck me then that he didn't care if anything happened to me. He just wanted the ride home. "I'm not giving you a ride after school," I shouted after him.

That day I rode home alone for the first time since I'd started school. The quiet of the mountains felt eerie, and at every bend in the road I thought a black car would come gliding out towards me. I regretted not waiting for Paco, but the sun was bright and no car appeared. I was almost back at the point where the paved road met the mountain path when two young goats chased each other onto the road in front of me. I swerved, screaming, and almost went into the ditch. The old goatherder lifted his cane and scolded his goats with a chattering sound that echoed behind me.

I was still feeling shaky as I drove into the square. I couldn't believe my eyes when I saw the black car with the dark windows parked in front of Montilla's house. I circled around the square, wondering if anyone was inside. The door to Montilla's house opened, and he stepped out with two older men in Civil Guard uniforms. I stopped beside Antonio's café to watch. He walked them to the car and bade them goodbye. His wooden movements reminded me of an old Frankenstein monster.

Montilla walked back towards his front door. When he was halfway up the path, he called over his shoulder as if he had been watching me all the time, "Miss Ana, come in. I have something for you."

Startled, I tried to say I was expected by Eleanor for lunch, but he seemed to anticipate an excuse. "It will only take a moment."

I left my bike outside his house so that people would know where I'd last been if I didn't come out. Montilla held the door open and I entered the gloomy vestibule of his fortress. There were no pretty mosaic tiles here like in Eleanor's home, no plants and birds. Everything was covered in plain brown tiles and scrubbed clean. I could smell disinfectant. Through double doors, I saw an enormous fireplace, and above it a framed row of medals hanging from bright ribbons. He picked up a page on a side table. "Do you recognize this?" he asked as he handed it to me.

I unfolded the paper. It was the first letter from Flaco, the fake one that had been written by the postal clerk. Where was the second one? When I looked up, I caught him watching me. "Where'd you get this?" I asked.

"I'm afraid I must have brushed it off the counter the

other day at the churros stall."

"Where's the other one?"

"Other one?"

It felt like a game of cat and mouse. "There were two letters."

"This is the only letter I found. My condolences on the loss of the other letter." He didn't sound even slightly sorry.

"That's okay, it wasn't important anyway," I bluffed.

He smiled. A nasty smile, big wooden teeth in the face of a strange marionette. "You are playing with fire. And everyone knows when children play with fire, they burn down houses – and if they're not careful, they hurt themselves."

I stuffed the letter in my pocket. I didn't like Montilla's threats – they seemed to be followed up by real coincidences: *Watch the mountain roads, it's a long way down* had been followed by the car almost forcing me off the road. The visit was over, and he pointed me towards the door.

I let myself out and took my motorbike home. I was pretty sure that Flaco's letter was one of the papers Montilla had burned – and in his own creepy way, he'd just let me know it. It was like he wanted me to know he could do whatever he wanted.

Finding Luis wasn't like looking for a peanut balanced on the edge of a drainpipe. This was serious stuff. My

great-uncle had disappeared. People were trying to drive me off the road. I was being threatened. I suddenly thought of all the things I hadn't done yet in my life: I hadn't water-skied or parachuted or gone on "The Bat" roller coaster; I hadn't had enough banana splits; I hadn't had enough pyjama parties. My life hadn't even started, and I didn't want it to end.

I sat in my gloomy cave and barred the door. I couldn't talk to Eleanor because then she would know I'd lost the letter. In the tunnels, the currents of wind that always drifted through made clunking noises, and I wondered if there was any chance the tunnels connected with Montilla's house.

I reached for a stack of my mom's blank postcards, and before I knew it, I had filled four.

Dear Mom and Dad,
Spain has been…interesting. I've learned to say everyday things in Spanish, like "okay" instead of "in accordance with your wishes," but the kids at school still giggle a lot when I talk. There's only a week left, it's gone by fast and, in a nutshell, I think I'm ready to come home. If a flight can't be arranged for today, tomorrow would be fine.

You see, I think I'm in grave danger. There's a weird

ex-Guardia – I'm sure his body is made of wood and only his head is alive (ughh!) – who doesn't like me because he thinks I'm snooping in his business. Which I am. I mean, I was. But I swear I won't any more. Because he probably kidnapped and murdered Luis – or something equally terrible.

So here I am in my room, and I can hear the wind, and I'm just wondering if the tunnels in this house might connect to his, and I was almost driven off the road today on the way to school. AND *I've lost something that's very important! If I'm sounding kinda hysterical, it's because* I AM*. And I really, really mean it, I want to come home.*

I know you don't think I'm thinking clearly 'cause I'm upset, so I just wanted to say that I sat down and thought carefully about this, and considered all sides of the situation, and I feel that it would be a prudent and smart thing to come home. I'll explain everything when I see you.

Love, Ana.

I stamped the postcards and ran out to the square and pushed them in the slot of the postal box. As soon as they left my fingers, I realized I'd forgotten to number them. I bit my lip. Now they *would* think I wasn't thinking clearly and they might make me stay. I hoped the postcards wouldn't get separated. It would be strange to get them out of order.

NINE

WHEN I SAT DOWN TO FACE ELEANOR'S ARMY, I WAS still rattled from my encounter with the car and Montilla. My plan was to isolate her king behind her army, which had advanced against me. I would corner her with my bishop and knight, and then I'd move in to checkmate. My bishop was in place, five diagonal squares away. Now to charge with my knight.

"Check," I said triumphantly.

"Well, well, still got some fight in you." She moved her king back a space.

I had to get her cornered in stalemate in the next couple of moves, before she turned her army around and surrounded me.

I brought a pawn forward which would cut off one of her king's escape routes. I thought I knew what she would do next, but instead of moving her rook forward to protect her king, Eleanor moved a pawn down towards my end of the board. It surprised me. I looked around the board. It would take me...I counted...three moves to get to checkmate. She had only one move left to get her pawn to my end of the board. Then she could get her queen back. How could I have missed that little pawn?!

Her queen came on the board and towered over my attack formation. In the next move, she seized my knight.

"No way!" I yelled.

"I'm afraid so."

I was in a corner now, my small army divided by the queen. "Look at my army! This is pathetic!"

"I'd say you're at around 1938. Sometime in the spring. The part of Spain you still control has been cut in half. The Nationals sit in the middle." She touched her queen. "They have new planes and tanks from their allies."

"I need a miracle," I complained.

"You still hold Madrid, against all odds. That's a miracle. You have volunteers from around the world willing to die for the workers and peasants of Spain. That's a miracle too."

I couldn't help feeling gloomy. My big attack had ended up being like an insect bite against Eleanor's army.

As though she read my thoughts, Eleanor said, "Every victory is important, no matter how small."

THE LAST DAY OF SUMMER SCHOOL came faster than I thought it would. The mornings in school had been good, after all. I was used to hearing kids speak and I didn't sound like I came from another century any more.

I'd been careful coming and going to school, often riding off the road where no car could drive. The day was beautiful, and I was tempted to skip the last dreary class of the summer. I was almost at the fork in the road that would take me up the mountain when I saw Paco walking ahead. I hadn't been riding home with him, and I missed hanging out with him. I hesitated, then drove up behind him and beeped the horn.

"Hola, Paco," I called. "You coming?"

He waved me on.

"Come on," I insisted.

He turned off the road and clambered up the hill towards the ridge. As I watched his back climb away from me, I realized that this was the end of our friendship. "You're not my friend," I yelled after him.

Paco turned around in surprise. "What's the matter?"

"You're not my friend." I turned the motorbike and drove away.

"Stop, Ana! Ana!" Paco scrambled down the hill. I could tell he was going to try to cut me off by running through the fields while I took the road circling the hill. I drove quickly and passed the gate just before he reached it. He threw his bag aside and chased me, calling my name.

I slowed down a little, letting him get closer.

"Where are you going?" he panted.

"None of your business."

"What about school?"

"I'm not going," I decided suddenly.

"Me neither!" He tried to grab the back of my shirt, and I accelerated out of his reach. "Ana," he pleaded.

I sped up a steep incline and stopped at the top, looking down at him standing out of breath on the road.

"You never play with me when your friends are around," I said.

"I do."

"No, you don't."

"You don't play soccer," he said, and when I tossed my head impatiently, he added, "I want to be your friend."

He started up the incline. When he was halfway up, I released the brakes and rolled past him down the hill.

"I'm sorry, Ana," he called after me. "Come eat at my house."

I stopped at the bottom. "When?"

"Today.... Will you come?" he asked.

"Maybe."

He started down the hill. "Wait for me, okay?"

I nodded, but when he came close, I drove off. I slowed

down and sped up along the road, laughing as he tried to catch me. He was laughing too, and eventually I let him catch me.

Pepe drove by just as Paco was getting on behind me. He had his taxi sign off and scaffolding boards lashed to the roof of his car. His half-open trunk was stacked full of buckets of whitewash paint. He stopped, and his three sons looked out at us from the back seat. Pepe winked. "Your boyfriend?" he asked.

"Friend," I said.

"Yeah? Maybe you want to go out with my boy?" Pepe reached back and tapped his youngest son's head. The other boys in the car laughed, and I blushed.

"Forget it, she's my girlfriend," Paco said.

"You see?" Pepe laughed and sped off, the boards rattling on his roof.

Paco and I drove up into the hills. It was a bright, warm day, and we lay on our backs and watched the clouds. I chewed on a stem of grass and wondered about what Paco had said. *Forget it, she's my girlfriend.* Had he just said that to get Pepe to leave? Before I could ask him, Paco rolled onto his elbow and plucked the grass from my lips. He tickled my throat with it, and when I tried to grab it back from him, I ended up in his arms. He threw away the grass and kissed me. His lips were soft.

I sat up in surprise and looked at him. He smiled,

then rolled over backwards down the hill. I laughed and started rolling after him. We rolled down one long slope after another until we were far below the road. By the time we climbed back up, the sun was beating on our backs and it was midday. The motorbike was surrounded by goats. Paco rushed into their midst and made them scatter. Behind him I could see the goatherder in the shade of a tree watching us.

I dropped Paco off outside the market so he could help his father close the stall, while I went home and told Eleanor about the lunch invitation. At two o'clock, I crossed the square to Paco's house. I was nervous, but he was waiting for me with the door open. He took my hand and led me across a large, unpaved courtyard where their market truck was parked. I could see a line of washing, partly concealed by an L-shaped wall. Sitting in the shade was an old man who gave me a toothless smile. Paco called him *"tío,"* which meant he was an uncle – or maybe a great-uncle by the look of him.

"Quién es?" Tío pointed to me, curious to know who I was.

"Ana."

"Extranjera," he said, looking me over. Foreigner.

Paco led me through another doorway into a patio where a large table was set for lunch. Tío was carried in on his chair by Paco's oldest brother and his father.

Behind the kitchen, I could see a caged room where their guard dogs paced back and forth, smelling the food and whining for their own meal. Paco's mother served heaping bowls of sausage stew. She had big fleshy arms and a strong back, and she never stopped adding food to everyone's plate. Every time I looked away, there was another piece of bread or spoonful of salad in front of me.

After lunch, Paco left the table to help his father and brothers unload some supplies from the truck. His mother and grandmother and the wives of his older brothers got up to clean the lunch dishes, and Tío and I were left at the table.

"Your skin is very white," he said. "Not many like you here."

"No," I agreed.

"No, there aren't," he repeated. "You and Paco play together?"

"Yes."

Paco was nowhere to be seen. I looked at the walls, decorated with plates and old photos. There was a picture of a group of men in a field standing by a donkey. And a yellowed picture of a soldier.

"Is that you?" I pointed to the photograph.

"Graciela's brother." He pointed to the kitchen at Paco's grandmother. "He's dead."

"Oh."

"Died when he was eighteen." He shook his head.

I sat up in my chair. If that was the brother of Paco's grandmother, and he'd died when he was eighteen, then he must have been a soldier in the civil war.

"Did you know him?"

"Oh, yeah." He settled back in his chair. "He didn't like the army clothes, said they were cut badly. He was a dandy. He polished his nails with oil before he went out." He held out sun-crinkled hands. "Not me."

"Did you know Luis Garcia?" I asked.

"Who?"

"Garcia. Luis Garcia," I repeated. If he'd grown up here, he must have known Luis.

Tío didn't answer.

"He was a soldier. He was the brother of Alfonso Garcia. They used to live in Sierra," I prompted.

"In Sierra...." Tío's face furrowed as he retreated into his memories. "That was long ago. Alfonso left. Where did he go? To France...? Yes, maybe France."

"Did you see his brother Luis before he disappeared?"

A mask fell across his face. "It was long ago." He rapped the floor with his cane and shouted to the kitchen.

"Wait, Tío!" the women yelled back.

"Did you ever see Luis?" I made a last try.

"Alfonso went away."

"Not Alfonso. Luis, his brother."

"What are you, a spy?" Paco's grandmother had come in behind me. I turned around and was startled by the hardness in her face. "You were sent by the old woman."

"What?"

"Yes, she sent you. She sent you to make friends with Paco and come here and spy." Her eyes were filled with hate.

"No!" I was shocked.

"Luis had ice in his veins, not blood like a decent person. He was the devil himself. He was a murderer." Paco's grandmother was so worked up that she was almost choking on the words as they came out.

"What's happening?" Paco's mother came out, looking between us.

"The girl has tricked us!"

"What?!" Her lungs had all the power of a market seller. "Are you slandering my family!?" She didn't wait for an answer. The look on Paco's grandmother's face was enough for her. "Get out! And don't ever come back here!"

My face burned as I got up. She yelled so loud I thought the whole village could hear. "And stay away from Paco!"

I ran through the courtyard, my heart pounding. Paco came out. We looked at each other with bewilderment.

"What is it?" I asked him.

"Go away."

"What's wrong, Paco? Tell me!"

"Go away, go away."

What was going on? Flaco had written that Luis was a person who loved smelling flowers and watching clouds, someone who couldn't fight. How could he be a cold-blooded murderer so hated by this family that just the mention of his name had me thrown out?

TEN

I RAN INTO THE HOUSE TO LOOK FOR ELEANOR, BUT I couldn't find her in the sitting room or her study. I was on my way to the kitchen when I met Amalia leading a man carrying a doctor's bag to the door.

"I have to talk to Eleanor, where is she?"

"She is sick," she stroked my head. "You eat with me in the kitchen tonight."

"What's wrong with her?"

"The hot summer is not good for her."

I sat at the kitchen table while Amalia prepared supper, and tried to put together everything I knew. Luis was a boy in the army who couldn't fight. He was last seen by his best friend, Flaco, when he was taken away from the front line because he had malaria. That had been six months before the war ended. And then he had vanished. Paco's grandmother said Luis was a murderer. Who did he kill? She said I was a spy, sent by Eleanor. But what would I be trying to find out? And then there was the letter from Flaco that said the *Guardia Civil* really wanted Alfonso. Why? He was the next person to find out about, I decided.

"Did you know Alfonso?" I asked Amalia.

"I knew them both since I was a girl. After the war, they left France and came to Belgium, where they lived with my family for a year. They were sick when they came from the concentration camp. And skinny. I remember I came into the room when Eleanor was changing one day and she had big purple spots on her legs – you know, scurvy? – and when they bit into food, their gums bled. But they were good people. Even when they were hungry, they told Mama to serve the children first. We were nine brothers and sisters.

"Alfonso liked to talk to people. He found himself a good suit and he made a business. He was good with other exiles. He started to help Jews who had diamonds to sell. Soon they found their own apartment, and together they learned the diamond business.

"They did well with their business, but in his heart Alfonso was always a revolutionary. He helped many people. He paid the mortgage on my parents' house. With nine children, they were poor. There was no money for the three youngest – my two brothers and me – for school. They paid for us. I went to learn *pâtisserie.*"

"Ah-ha! That's why you bake like you do."

She smiled. "When I finished, I could have worked in a bakery, but I wanted to cook for them. I knew they needed help. Alfonso came out of the concentration camp very weak, and later he got tuberculosis. Eleanor couldn't do everything on her own."

"Why didn't she go back to Canada?"

"She promised Alfonso she wouldn't stop looking for Luis. When he died, she closed the business in Antwerp and came back to his village. When she bought this house, she said to me that she wouldn't leave without finding Luis. But nobody wanted to talk. The village records showed nothing. It was a waste to come here." She slapped the dough she was working roughly.

The house was dull with Eleanor in bed. Amalia said we should just let her rest, but we stayed close to home in case she needed us, and to pass the time, we baked pastries, enough to feed the village. At night we watched old black-and-white Hollywood movies on TV. Amalia ate cake and smiled along with the characters and cried at the sad parts. I sat with her and giggled whenever a new movie started, because the dubbed Spanish voices were always the same, no matter who the American actors were in the movies.

Our quiet days didn't last long. The villagers were getting ready for a weekend holiday, and there was a lot of activity outside our door as the square was decorated with lights and paper flowers. From the balcony I saw Antonio setting up extra tables outside his café. At night the street was full of people singing and clapping. Every balcony around the square was filled with families watching the festivities below. A group of local musicians played marching music, and couples danced on the paved patio around the fountain.

I sat on the balcony and saw Cricket drop something into a big jug of wine punch called *sangría*. It looked like a torpedo was circling the rim of the jug, then a small frog leaped out. Cricket scrambled to catch it, but before he could put it in again, his mother swept him up in her arms and swung him around to the music. I saw Paco with his brothers and friends, a large group of them walking slowly around the square. I tried to look away, but couldn't stop watching him.

Amalia came up with a tray of desserts. Her hair was coiled in a bun, and she wore lipstick. She leaned against the rail, looking out. Antonio waved up at her, and she waved back. There was so much music and celebration below that we didn't notice the two uniformed Civil Guards approaching the house until we heard them pounding on the door.

Amalia went downstairs, and I leaned over the balcony to see who was there. When I saw the black hats of the Civil Guard, my breath caught in my throat. Were they after me? I ran down to the front door and stood in the shadows, listening.

"...the Señora is too ill to be disturbed," Amalia was insisting.

Behind the officers, people were gathering to listen. "We have a report that you have been here illegally for three years. You are a citizen of Belgium." The officer who spoke was polite but formal, leaving no doubt about the seriousness of the discussion. His partner stayed silent and watchful beside him. It felt like icy fingers were crawling up my arms, leaving a trail of goosebumps. I recognized the heavy-set faces of these two men – they were the Civil Guards who'd left Montilla's house the day I was there! I pushed further back into the shadows.

"I know my papers are in order. She always makes sure," Amalia said.

"What do you do here?"

"I work for the señora."

"Then where's your work permit?"

"Work permit! Work permit!" I could hear the word rippling back through the crowd.

"I've already told you. She has all the papers, but she is sick."

The officers didn't seem to care. "Bring your papers to us by Tuesday morning – residency and work permit. Tuesday morning, or we'll be back."

When Amalia closed the door, I stepped out of the shadows. "What is it?" I asked.

She was perplexed. "I don't know...I think someone has made a report against me."

"About what?"

"That I'm here illegally."

"Is that true?"

"No, but I can't prove anything until Eleanor is better."

I was worried. If Eleanor wasn't strong enough to look for Amalia's papers, what would happen? When the *Guardia* came back, would they take her away? Would they make her leave the country? Maybe I could find Amalia's papers. I went back up to the library and started searching through stacks of paper.

There were pages with lists of names, embassies, and human rights groups that were crossed off. I wasn't interested in them, but there was a letter that caught my eye – because it was signed by Alfonso. Finally, the first evidence of him.

Dear Friends at Amnesty International:

My name is Alfonso Garcia. I was a soldier in the Republican army during the Spanish Civil War. I am looking for my brother, Luis Garcia, born in Sierra, Spain, on July 4, 1922.

In December, 1938, I learned that my brother had contracted malaria and was hospitalized at a medical unit in the San Rolando monastery. My fiancée went to see him there, since I couldn't go into the National zones. The hospital staff told her he was too sick to leave.

We had to leave Spain when Barcelona fell, and we've been trying to find Luis without success since then. His description is as follows.

Appearance: Black hair, brown eyes, glasses, recovering from malaria, weak and pale.

Height: Approx. 5´10˝.

Position: Infantryman in the National army.

I ask you to check his name against your list of exiles and to keep his data on file. I would be grateful for any information about his whereabouts.

Sincerely,
Alfonso Garcia

The National army was Franco's army. If Luis was fighting on the side of the Nationals that meant that he was fighting against his brother in the Republican army. How could that be?

ELEVEN

T HE NEXT MORNING, I OPENED THE DOOR TO Eleanor's bedroom a crack and peered in. I had never looked inside her room before. Her bed was like an old galleon ship, with thick posts of dark wood and a strange wooden skirt around it. She looked small lying in it. *There was an old woman who went to sea,* the nursery rhyme came into my head.

"Don't just stand there. Come in," she called out to me. She looked like she was in a bad mood.

"How are you feeling?"

"I don't want to talk about that!" She waved the subject away. "What happened last night?" she asked. "Something is wrong, but Amalia won't tell me. Treating me like a child!"

I told her about the visit from the Civil Guard.

"Of course her papers are in order. This is more nonsense from Montilla. I thought he'd stopped this long ago, but obviously he still feels the need to make us want to leave." Her eyes closed and she sank back into the pillows. "I will get up this afternoon and fix all this."

I waited, but she didn't say anything else and her breathing grew deep as if she was sleeping. I backed out of the room, and just as I was closing the door, she said, "Ana, keep an eye on things."

LATER IN THE MORNING, Amalia sent me out to the meadows at the top of the cliff to bring her some wild thyme. On my way back, I cut through the narrow passageway beside Montilla's house to save time. I was halfway down the passage when a figure blocked the light at the exit.

I stopped and my heart plunged into my stomach. Was this just a coincidence, or had someone been waiting for me? I couldn't tell who it was in the shade of the walls. If I turned around and retreated, the person might chase me, and behind the village there was only field and cliff and no one to help me. I kept walking. I could always push my way into the square. I could always scream my head off.

As I came closer, I saw it was a woman with a black shawl over her head. Even though I couldn't see her face,

I knew she was looking at me. She shifted her stocky body and blocked my path.

"We know things about you," a familiar voice hissed. "We know what your family did, and we do not forgive."

I looked at the mysterious covered head with my mouth open, too shocked to speak.

"Stay away from us and mind your own business," the woman said in a way that made my skin crawl. I tried to place her voice. It was someone I knew.

"What did my family do?" I managed to ask.

The question seemed to anger the woman. "Don't make trouble, or the same thing will happen to you that happened to Luis Garcia."

She pushed past me with surprising force, and my back hit the wall. I watched her silhouette move down the passageway, and it suddenly came to me who she was: Paco's grandmother, Graciela.

Something had happened during the war between Paco's family and mine, something that must have been terrible. Why else would I be getting all of these threats? I wanted to go home. I missed my parents and my room and the street we lived on. Had my postcards arrived? Were my parents getting ready to bring me home? I felt safest when I was close to Amalia, so I followed her around for the rest of the morning. She was in a quiet, worried mood herself. She mopped the kitchen silently and took the laundry outside to hang it up.

A door slid open to the house that shared the alley where the laundry lines were. I had a sense that someone had been watching and waiting. It was the neighbour's maid, Pilar. The family who lived here was away during the summer. They went to a villa by the sea, and Pilar stayed and tended the place for them. She eyed Amalia sharply, then launched into a stream of chatter.

"Amalia, did you see the Mayor dance?"

Amalia shook her head.

"I've never seen him dance before! He dances with his belly, and his wife is so far on the other side that she dances by herself. He was like this." She turned her laundry basket up against her stomach and danced with bow legs, her back arched, making the plastic lattice jut out.

I laughed, and even Amalia smiled.

Pilar took this as encouragement and pressed on. "You going to the market now, Amalia?"

"Later."

"I'm going with you. Come by, okay? I have to show you the figs. Eduardo has a special pile, but he only gives them to me. I'll take you there and we'll get some for you, okay?"

Amalia nodded reluctantly. Pilar wasn't going to take no for an answer. We finished the laundry and collected our shopping bags. Pilar latched on to Amalia's arm the minute they started walking. I tagged along behind, trying to catch the stream of words Pilar was hissing into Amalia's ear. "...never, never, never would they send you away!...not over Antonio's dead body...and mine!"

At the market, the fruit sellers gave Amalia fruit from the front of their displays. Usually they put their best fruit in the front and then filled their paper cones with fruit of lesser quality from behind. The woman at the cheese stall charged her less than the scale showed. Everyone wanted to know what the Civil Guard wanted. I hovered in the background, gathering intelligence.

As we walked through the market, the advice Amalia got was more far-fetched with every person she talked to. Someone had a brother-in-law in Madrid who was a clerk in the Traffic and Parking department and could fix this; someone else knew someone who had written to the king of Spain and he had personally given them permission to stay in Spain; and the owner of the olive stand told Amalia that she had a connection with a fortune teller who had special powers to change things.

THE NEXT MORNING, the village turned out early in a long line, even before the oil had heated. Antonio came to the back door as always, but he was fidgety and kept putting his hands in his pockets and taking them out. "Amalia, I know you're in trouble, and I have to speak to you."

"What is it, Antonio?"

The line of customers pushed forward around the window to listen.

Antonio looked very nervous and not like himself at all. He stuttered as he spoke. "Will you m-m-marry me?"

Amalia smiled gently. "Thank you, Antonio." She took his hands and he held on, waiting. "You're a good friend to help, but I think the Señora will find my papers...so you don't have to make this sacrifice...."

"No," he said, "no, no...I mean, even if they find your papers, I...I want to marry you." His eyes were watering, as if he was melting from inside.

Amalia's smile grew brighter as they gazed at each other. Someone at the window sighed dreamily. Amalia and Antonio fell into each other's arms and kissed for what seemed to me an awfully long time. Cheers erupted from the crowd, and Antonio announced that everything was on the house.

I went back to the house with a tray of churros and hot chocolate to report to Eleanor, who I found sitting up in her bed.

"What happened today?" she asked.

"Antonio kissed Amalia." I couldn't help smiling.

"Well, it's about time." She dunked her churros into

her hot chocolate and took a big bite. "Mind you, now he'll want to take her away from me." She sighed, but didn't look too upset as she devoured her breakfast. She was finally getting over her heat fatigue, I observed with relief.

Now all of the questions I'd had from the strange events of the week came back. "Eleanor, why were Luis and Alfonso fighting against each other?"

"They weren't."

"But Alfonso was with the Republicans and Luis was with the Nationals."

"You have to understand what civil war is like. Spain was split in pieces. Every time Franco won a new territory, it was cut off from the rest. No mail, no news, no food or supplies could get through. Alfonso was fighting for the Republicans, and Luis was too young to be in the army when the war started. He stayed home with his mother and sister, your grandmother, Consuelo. They all went to stay with an aunt who lived in Almeria. She had a bakery, so at least there was always a bit of bread to eat.

"Almeria was taken by Franco and cut off from the rest of the Republican territory, and Luis was drafted into Franco's army. Like all the other boys, he didn't know anything about war or soldiering. Alfonso was beside himself when he found out. But by that time his work for the Republicans made it impossible for him to even think of crossing the lines."

"Was Montilla after Alfonso too?"

"Yes, he was after anyone who was against Franco. And Alfonso was a greater threat than most because he was a revolutionary. He believed in equality for all men. He fought with his heart and was very good at what he did. This made him dangerous to Franco."

"Paco's grandmother called me a spy and told me never to come back to their house."

There was a beat of silence. "Did she?"

I explained my conversation with Tío, and how Paco's grandmother had reacted. "Why would she say Luis was a murderer?"

"I don't know, but I have always suspected that family knows more about his disappearance than they let on."

"Definitely, they do. Graciela cornered me yesterday and told me to get my nose out of her business." I knew now that Graciela and Montilla were on the same side. I'd watched Montilla's house from the library balcony and noticed that no one else brought him gifts or groceries. In fact, most people seemed to avoid him. But Paco came three times a week, always early before anyone was in the square.

Eleanor looked at me thoughtfully, "I had a letter from your parents."

"Oh yeah?" I tried to sound casual.

"They say you want to go home." She sounded disappointed.

"Well, I'd want to stay if everyone wasn't so nasty and suspicious – I mean, now I don't have Paco as a friend, and Montilla tried to kill me –"

"What!"

I slapped my hand over my mouth. How did that get out? Now I would have to tell her about the letter.

"Well...you see, I did something really stupid.... I...I lost Flaco's letters and Montilla found them." Eleanor's eyes widened. "He gave me back one of the letters, but I think he burned the real letter from Flaco and his son. And I panicked and I wrote my parents saying I wanted to come home." It was all spilling out. "Because I didn't dare tell you what a big mess I'd made of everything. I'm so sorry," I finished.

I waited for Eleanor to yell at me for the letter, for having lost her precious evidence, for having been careless. But instead, she leaned her head back and said, "So, you've made yourself a target too. What is it in the Garcia blood? If there's a bull in sight, you'll find a red cape."

"I'd get the letter back for you if I could," I said miserably.

"Forget it! The letter is the least of our worries."

I sighed with relief. The worst was over. I didn't have to hide anything from Eleanor any more. In fact, everything was different now. Eleanor was getting better, all was out in the open, and I was on the trail to finding Abuela's brother.

I didn't need to go home now. I didn't even want to.

"I'll contact your parents to make arrangements for you to go home," Eleanor said. "I don't think it's safe for you to be here any more."

TWELVE

AT NIGHT I LAY ON MY BED, STARING AT THE SHAFT CUT into the cliff wall. How could I convince Eleanor and my parents that I wanted to stay now? I had to start putting the pieces of this puzzle together soon, or my only chance to find Luis would be gone.

I went through all of the village faces I knew: who might know something, who was friendly and open, who wasn't. I began drifting off to sleep when I saw a face flicker through the others. I couldn't place it; it was like trying to remember a word that was on the tip of my tongue. My heart started racing. I knew if I could see this face, it would be the person who could tell me something. It was someone I had overlooked. Someone everyone had overlooked. I sat up when I realized who it was.

It was hard to sleep after that. Before dawn I went into

the kitchen, broke a long loaf of bread in half, cut a slab of cheese, wrapped it all in a towel, and quietly walked my motorbike out of the patio.

The streets were deserted, but at the marketplace vendors were setting up for the day. I saw Paco and his brothers unloading meat from their truck. Paco watched me approach. He wore stained blue overalls, and his eyes were tired.

I stopped across the street from him. He turned his back to me, hoisted a leg of pork to his shoulder, and carried it into the market. I waited until he came back out.

"Paco."

"Go away."

"Paco, I just want to find my uncle."

"I hope he's lost forever."

"He was a good person."

"If you think that, then you're as rotten as he was."

"Don't you want to know the truth?"

"I already know it."

"Come on, Paco, stop daydreaming." Paco's father yelled from the stall. "We have to pick up another load."

Paco disappeared into the truck, and I continued on my way.

The road ended at a ruin of a house. I tried to ride through the stony fields above, but was soon forced to abandon the bike and go on by foot. In the distance, I

saw the flicker of a fire. I bunched up the bread and cheese and scrambled up the hill. The goatherder must have seen me from far below, but he kept his head down and tended to his fire. His goats were lying under a cluster of low trees, and it was a serene scene. I felt as if I was walking into a private, hidden room, though we were out in the open air.

I stopped in front of him and held out my package of food. He looked at me, then away, and tapped the ground with his stick. I put the bread and cheese down and, after standing a while, crouched down beside it. I unwrapped the towel, wishing I'd taken a few more treats from Amalia's cupboards. He watched while I tore myself a piece of bread and cut off a chunk of cheese. I held out the knife, which he accepted in his dirty, sunburned hands. His face was wrinkled by the sun and the wind, his hair was almost white, and his back was bent. We sat in silence for a long time. He didn't look at me as he ate.

"Was that your house?" I pointed to the ruin down the hill.

He shook his head.

"Where do you live?"

He waved his hand vaguely towards my back. I turned around. All I could see were hills streaked with grey rocks.

"Were you here during the war?" The question didn't seem to make sense to him. "Were you here," I circled around the hills with my arms, "when you were a boy?"

My voice was a bit shaky. I was excited. I'd seen him and his goats everywhere in the hills and along the roads. He would know this countryside better than anyone. And if his family had kept goats, he would know what happened that spring when the war ended.

"I was with my father."

"Your father had goats?"

He nodded.

"So you saw the fighting."

He didn't seem to understand.

"You saw what happened." I looked down the hills and ribbons of roads below and confirmed, half to myself, "Yes, you see everything from here."

When I looked back, I caught him watching my face with amusement, as if I'd opened a secret door. He averted his eyes.

"What did you see when you were a child?"

He shrugged his shoulders.

"Did you see soldiers? Maybe hiding? Maybe a boy hiding?"

"A boy?"

"Yes, a big boy."

"I saw the boys." He thought for a while. "I saw the generals, the captains." He looked at the fire. "They couldn't build a fire, there was no wood." Even now the hills were stony and had only a few shrubs growing on them.

"What else did you see?" I tried to contain a smile of excitement. This might be the right lead, finally!

"They brought water in trucks. Both sides had a hill. The Nationals there. The Reds there. They shouted at each other through big cones. One side was full of men who spoke a different tongue. They didn't have blankets even." He stopped and chewed on some bread. It took a while, since he didn't have many teeth left.

"Did boys fight here?"

He continued talking as if he hadn't heard my question. "At night they crawled on their bellies into the farmers' fields and stole all of the potatoes," he said. "They didn't even fight, they were too busy trying to stay warm and get food. Sometimes they shot their guns at nothing. They killed two goats like that – out of stupidity." He was quiet, as if this was all he had to say on the subject.

"The boy I'm looking for is Luis Garcia. Did you see him?"

"There were many boys."

"He was from the village. His brother Alfonso was from there too."

"He went home."

"No." I shook my head, disappointed. "That's not the boy."

"Yes, yes, that's the boy," he insisted.

"No, no. He didn't go home, he disappeared."

"After."

"After what?"

"After he went home, they threw stones at him. Then he went away."

"What?"

The goatherder waved in the direction of the village. "It was near the end and everyone knew Franco was winning. They were crazy."

"What happened?"

"They threw stones," he repeated, "and garbage, and sticks."

"At Luis?"

He nodded.

I could hardly breathe. This was the end of my path, unexpectedly. "Did he die?"

"My father found him in a field. He said the war had made people crazy. *Enough is enough,* he said. *Enough!*" He said it as if he saw his father standing before him shouting against the insanity of the war.

"And then?"

"My father carried him home. The stones hurt his head. He thought his mother was in the room, and he talked to her all the time. He thought his brother was coming for him, and he sat by the door and waited."

"Did anyone in the village report it to the Civil Guard?"

He dismissed the question with a wave. "There was no law."

"What about Montilla?"

"Montilla came after the war was over. They made him Chief of Police. But by then Luis knew how to hide. He stayed in the caves on the other side. Then, after a while..." he thought about it, "after a while, he left."

The sun was growing hot, and the veils of mist had lifted off the hills. The goatherder got up and talked to his goats with the special sounds he had for them. I stayed watching the smoking embers of the fire. So Montilla didn't get Luis – the villagers did.

I hurried home to share the news with Eleanor.

THIRTEEN

Eleanor gave me a cold look of warning. "This new information is from a source you are sure of?"

"Yes."

A flicker of apprehension crossed her face. "Go on then."

I told her about my visit to the goatherder. "I don't know how long Luis was hiding in those caves, but Montilla never found him! And no one knows where he went afterwards."

Eleanor stood up, electrified. "We have to find those caves."

"I think I know where they might be." I'd noticed the cliffs on the other side of the valley on my rides through the mountains.

"Then let's get ready," she said. "Follow me." Eleanor

led me up to the library. She pulled one book after another off the shelves. "Here we are: *Forensic Evidence: Collection and Interpretation;* read through that and I think this will be helpful, though it might be a bit out-dated and relating more to archeology, no...let's not waste time on that." She was flushed, and her step had a spring that made her stumble over her cane.

"You see, many locations don't have visible clues. Do you understand?" She looked at me keenly and continued before I could answer. "You have to learn to recognize a clue. Many people walk past the most flagrant clues because they don't know what to look for. You see? When you enter that cave, you must be able to first of all recognize what you are looking at. There may be a few remains that will tell you how long Luis lived there. For example, how deep are the ashes in the firepit? How black are the stones around it? You see? How did he live? Did he manage to have anything from the house? Did he leave a message in the cave? Did he leave a marker of sorts that showed the direction he headed in?"

She went on, losing me in a web of questions. I busied myself with putting together a forensic kit, which made her happy. When I finished, my canvas bag held cotton gloves, small plastic bags with labels, plastic containers, a soft, wide brush, a flashlight, and a camera.

We left early in the afternoon. Eleanor insisted on

taking the motorbike. She didn't know who to trust in the village and didn't even want Pepe to drive her. "Not until we know more," she said. She sat carefully behind me, her cane hooked over her arm. Amalia had refused to help with any of the preparations, saying it was too dangerous for Eleanor to go to some mysterious caves – and riding on the back of a motorbike! She stood with her arms folded and watched disapprovingly as we drove out of the courtyard.

We took the road down into the valley, circling around the base of the wide cliffs and going around to the other side, where we discovered a honeycomb of dark mouths close to the top of the ridge. How could we get to them?

In the end, I found a steep dirt road that I drove along slowly. I had to put my feet down often to keep the bike from falling over. Finally, we reached the top, and I parked close to the edge. We walked over and looked down. The rock face fell away to a long vertical drop below. There was a narrow footpath, more like a ledge, that led in the direction of the caves. I swung my leg over a low traffic barrier and prepared to inch my way along it.

"Ana," Eleanor stopped me with her hand on my shoulder. I looked back and saw her eyes on the steep drop below. "I don't think I can let you do this."

"I'm okay," I reassured her. "I think this leads right to

the cave. It's so wide I don't even have to walk sideways along it. Let me try."

She released my shoulder. "Be careful."

I walked carefully along the rock ledge until I came to the opening. Cool air met me at the mouth of the cave. I stepped inside. The light fell away almost at once, and the darkness beyond the entrance was impenetrable. My knees went weak. I took the flashlight out of my shoulder bag and turned it on. A small circle of light fell on the dirt floor. The darkness was still everywhere around me like a mouth waiting to swallow me. I stepped back into the sunshine, my skin ridged with goosebumps, and started to climb back up to Eleanor. My hands were shaky and I didn't even realize that I was still holding my flashlight until it slipped out of my grasp and tumbled far below, where it smashed on the rocks.

"I can't do it," I told her when I got back up.

"The heights?" she asked, worried.

"The dark."

"Oh, it's just air," she was relieved. "Use your flashlight."

I shook my head. "I dropped it. Anyway, I can't. I just can't. I feel like I'm going to be smothered," I admitted with embarrassment.

"But there's nothing there."

"Sorry," I said, and couldn't suppress a shiver when I

thought of the dank cave.

"This is a quandary," Eleanor muttered.

We sat on the hill in gloomy silence. We were so close. The answer to fifty years of searching might be right underneath us. If Paco and I were still friends, he would go in there with me. I dismissed the thought.

The sun lowered in a blazing, yellow ball, level with our eyes. Eleanor adjusted her hat to shield her eyes, then gasped and got to her feet faster than I'd ever seen her move.

"Ana, Ana! Now. Quickly!" She walked to the edge and looked down. "Look, the sun is in line with the cave. You've got seven minutes, maybe ten or fifteen. It should be as light in there as if there was an electric bulb on. Go!"

I scrambled down, and to my amazement, the cave was flooded with dusty yellow light. It was enough to get me inside, and I entered like a mortal going into a den of vampires. The sinking globe at my back was my final protection, and I knew I had to hurry. I crawled on my hands and knees, running my hands over the surface of the ground, disturbing silken sheets of dirt, forcing myself into the dark recesses by the walls and towards the back of the cave where it was barely lit.

I sang nursery rhymes at the top of my lungs, ones I didn't remember knowing. My knees wobbled in fear and took a beating as I darted around the rocky floor. Anything solid that my hand came across was thrown into a pile by the front without second thought. The cotton gloves, the labelled bags and brushes, stayed in my canvas bag. There was no marking where things had been found, no reconstructing the living conditions.

The automatic camera stayed around my wrist, forgotten, flopping around on the ground. It accidentally rolled under my hand in my dash around the cave and when my weight came down on it, it flashed, blinding me. All I could see was an electric-green haze. I sat back on my heels and blinked, trying to get my sight back. All of a sudden I felt my back grow cold.

The light in the cave had been sucked out, and I knew the sun had lowered behind the hills. I swept the pile and a good sackful of dirt into my canvas pack and backed out hastily, almost falling down the steep cliff, my senses in a jumble. I crawled up the ledge, my legs unable to hold me, and lay on the grass, shivering with cold in the sunshine.

Eleanor patted my back and shouted, "Bravo! Tough girl! Brave girl!"

"I was terrified!" I complained loudly.

"There is bravery in your heart as surely as there is magma in the earth's core."

I rolled over. "Really?"

"Really," she said and hugged me.

Once we got home, the bagged goods were spilled out on the table. A couple of huge, dried beetles tumbled out that made me scream with repulsion. There was some half-burned wood, a piece of rusted metal with a point on the end that looked like an old can opener, lots of fine silt, and then something that made Eleanor gasp. A key. Long and flat. Not like any other key I'd seen.

"The key to the safety deposit box," she whispered and pressed it to her chest.

ELEANOR KEPT THE KEY IN HER POCKET, and I knew she was thinking about it, because every now and then she reached down to touch it. We were hunched over the chess game. I was in a pathetic situation. All I had left were four pawns, a knight, and, of course, my king.

"I guess this is the end," I said. I wished I'd been able to win the war.

"Close to the end," she agreed. "I'd say this is the fall of 1938. The Spanish government has called all foreign volunteers away from the front lines and sent them home. The Republicans know they've lost. There's no point sacrificing more lives." Her bishop took my last knight.

FOURTEEN

The next morning I found Eleanor sitting at the breakfast table, her teacup drained. "I've called a taxi for eight o'clock. You have ten minutes to eat if you want to come with me."

"Where are we going?" I asked, picking up a piece of toast and slipping an apple into my pocket.

"To Toledo, which is a good hour and a half away. The key you found yesterday belongs to a safety deposit box. I know that Alfonso did business at a bank there. Let's go and see what we can find out." She refilled her cup while I ate quickly.

"We'll spend the day in Toledo, anyway. It's a fascinating city, and you mustn't leave Spain without seeing it." The words hit me with a jolt. *You mustn't leave Spain without seeing it.* I only had a few days left. But I didn't want to go. We were too close to finding Luis.

Pepe came in his taxi. He sprang to open the door for us and didn't make any hissing noises at all. Eleanor must have been a special customer, because Pepe drove straight to Toledo without stopping once to pick up eggs or chat with owners of roadside cafés. As we approached, the buildings of Toledo were gilded in morning light, a fitting first sight of the city of gold.

When we got to the bank, it was already filled with lines of people, and it seemed we waited forever before we had a chance to present the key to the bank manager, a tall, well-dressed man whose aftershave preceded him into the room. He took the key and disappeared behind the counter, returning a few minutes later.

"The key is no longer valid," he said, handing it back to Eleanor.

"Did you look in the registry?"

"The box is not in the Garcia family name in the current book."

"And in the book before that?" she asked.

"We don't keep those records here." He was polite but uninterested.

"The box was never officially closed, and we must trace the contents," Eleanor insisted.

"The bank is not responsible for unclaimed contents."

"You don't just throw away the contents, do you?

People's valuables, their property deeds, their wills...." Her voice rose with each word.

Customers turned to listen. The bank manager's face grew red, and he assured her coldly that he would find any information he could. He asked that we return before the bank closed for lunch.

The wonders of Toledo made me forget about the safety deposit box. We visited the city's majestic cathedral with its vaulted walls and gold carvings, and walked through streets lined with old mansions that had studded, wooden doors protecting beautiful inner patios. When we arrived back at the modern, mirrored doors of the bank, I felt like I'd just travelled through time back to the present. A reflection in the glass caught my attention as I held the door open for Eleanor: a black car with dark windows was parked across the street. It was identical to the car that had tried to run me down. My stomach did a nervous flip.

Inside the bank, the manager ushered us into his office. "You must understand how difficult it is to trace unclaimed items from so long ago," he started. "It will take at least six weeks to get the records from Madrid."

"Impossible. We can't wait that long," Eleanor said.

"I don't know what the records will tell you anyway. I telephoned Mr. Costa, the retired manager who worked at the bank for forty years. He doesn't remember a thing."

He looked at us apologetically. "I've done all I can."

"Then I must speak with Mr. Costa," said Eleanor.

The bank manager paused, surprised. "I'm sorry, that is not possible."

"I am the only remaining member of the family in Spain. I haven't received anything from this bank. If the former bank manager will not see me, then I will take this matter to the police."

"The bank has acted properly." He was angry again.

"How can you be so certain when you have no answers yourself?"

He hesitated, "Will you be satisfied if you speak to Mr. Costa?"

It was Eleanor's turn to hesitate. If this was a dead end, she would have no other avenue to explore. "Yes," she decided.

He left us alone for a moment and came back with a name and address written on a card. "He has agreed to see you."

We thanked the manager and left his office. I looked across the road and saw that the car was still there. I stopped Eleanor before we reached the doors to the street. "Eleanor, I think we're being followed."

Fortunately, the mirrored windows of the bank protected us, because we could see out but they couldn't see in.

"By whom?" She seemed only mildly surprised.

"I don't know. But that's the car that tried to run me down, and I've seen it outside Montilla's house."

"Good. That means we're getting close if he's sending his goons out." She didn't seem half as worried as I was. "Let's go out the doors on the other side and get a taxi."

We managed to slip out unnoticed and hail a taxi. We gave the driver directions to Mr. Costa's house, asking him to drive quickly and make sure he wasn't followed.

Mr. Costa lived in a beautiful old building with a shaded courtyard. We went up an ancient elevator with an iron gate to the top floor and were let into a spacious apartment by a maid. An old man with thick glasses appeared. Even though it was hot outside, his apartment was cool, and he wore a wool cardigan and slippers. He didn't look like an important bank manager.

Mr. Costa invited us to have refreshments, and when we declined, he asked to hear our questions. We were relieved when he told us we were the first people to ask him about Luis. That meant we were a step ahead of Montilla.

Eleanor explained that the contents of the safety deposit box might lead us to Luis.

"How many years ago was that?" he asked.

"Sometime in 1940."

Mr. Costa raised his eyebrows and made a gesture of futility.

"It's important," Eleanor urged. "We lost him after the war, and he was very young."

"And you wait until now to come to me?"

"We've been looking for years, but I didn't know he had access to this box...."

"I am an old man. I have too much information already in my head, you know?" He tapped his temple. "All the cabinets are overflowing. How do you expect me to pull out a memory of a boy I might have seen for a few minutes once or twice a month?"

"Just tell me this, what did you do with unclaimed boxes?"

"We didn't have any unclaimed boxes."

"If you didn't, then you should remember the box that Luis had. He might have stopped paying for it...."

"Ah, that's another story. Yes, we did have boxes that people didn't pay for and if there was no money in the account to take for the box, we contacted the owners. This happened sometimes, yes." There was a pause. "What was his name?"

"Luis Garcia."

The old man sipped the cup of tea his maid had brought him. Then he shrugged his shoulders.

"He might have been dirty when he came in," I said, remembering the silt in the cave.

"Yes!" Eleanor agreed. "Yes, he might have been unshaven

and even in ragged clothes."

Mr. Costa's face changed. It grew guarded.

"You've remembered something!" she said.

"This was after the war. There were many people who were poor and hungry. They came in old clothes, they didn't have soap and razors, they didn't have food...."

"But?" Her eyes were locked on his face.

"There was a boy. He was thin and pale, like he was evaporating from hunger." He paused, then said significantly, "He had long hair."

"Yes, of course, he would." Eleanor was leaning forward and Mr. Costa was reluctantly letting her draw the story from him.

"So I knew that he was...a fugitive, or something. Maybe sick," he tapped his head, "maybe...a criminal."

"And?"

"He gave me the key to the box. I was surprised. I got the box for him and left him in a private cubicle with it. He was in there a long time. A long, long time. My assistant manager at the time had been a sergeant in Franco's army. He didn't like this boy with his long hair. He thought he might be planting a bomb or doing something...you have to think what it was like – everyone was suspected of being anti-Franco...so I called the police."

We gasped.

Mr. Costa looked at us with regret. "He came out

before the police arrived. The assistant manager tried to detain him, but he got away. He slipped out of his hold like a wild animal. The police looked everywhere for him. There were roadblocks even, and he was put on file."

"Why?!"

"Suspicious activities...." He opened his hands apologetically.

"So the police wanted to see what was inside the box," she prompted.

"Yes."

"What did they find?"

"I don't know...nonsense. Notes on paper. The police thought it was code, but they brought it back after a few months.... There was nothing of value, I assure you," he added, as if we might be looking for an inheritance.

"What did you do with it all?" she asked impatiently.

"We would have contacted the last address we had. There was a property deed, I think, and everything was returned to the owners."

When we finished with Mr. Costa, we went back into the centre of Old Toledo. As we'd arranged, Pepe was waiting for us outside the cathedral. He was brushing chicken feathers off the back seat, and I could hear clucks of distress in the trunk. He took us quickly out of Toledo.

The drive home was quiet. Eleanor and I were both deep in thought. I told myself that if the property deed was returned to the owners, Alfonso or Luis or Consuelo should have gotten it, but none of them had. Who then had the deed been returned to?

"Paco says his family is telling the truth about Luis," I said. I spoke freely, knowing that Pepe didn't understand English.

"Of course."

"But he's wrong! How can he defend their lies?!"

She studied me. "Because it's too hard for him to believe anything else."

"He shouldn't try to cover up the past," I insisted and suddenly felt angry. "I hate him."

"This has nothing to do with him. Or with you," she said, putting her hand on my arm when she saw me protest. "These are crimes of another generation. You mustn't carry on the bad feelings." She patted my hand. "Tonight I have to get my thoughts straight, and tomorrow we may finally have the answer I've been waiting for."

FIFTEEN

THE NEXT MORNING I WOKE UP TO THE SMELL OF Amalia's coffee wafting down the hall. I rolled out of bed and hurried into the shower. I didn't want to miss what was coming today.

I found Eleanor in the library, surrounded by her files and papers.

"How does one prepare oneself for an encounter such as this? With people who are neighbours, community members, and enemies at the same time – good and bad all rolled into one. Look at this." She dropped her hand on the files and a waft of dust escaped from the sides. "Fifty years of searching and the clues were under my nose."

I waited.

"The family home where your grandmother and her

brothers grew up is across the square. Many nights I've stood outside and watched it from the balcony. Number 19."

"Paco's house?!"

She nodded. "The house was never sold, and the records show that the property always belonged to Paco's family. By the time I arrived in Sierra, nobody wanted to talk about the property or the war. It was long over for them. I always thought that one day someone would slip up and give something away, or that something would reveal itself to me." She stood up. "And now it has, thanks to you."

"Are you going to see Paco's family?"

"Yes."

"They'll be nasty," I warned.

"Let's not procrastinate then," she said. "It won't get any easier to do."

We walked across the square and knocked on the large wooden doors that led into the courtyard. All remained silent, as if someone was hiding. It was Sunday. Eleanor rapped with her cane again, loudly. Finally, we heard the locks being pulled back, and the door swung open. It was Paco's oldest brother.

"I must speak with your father," Eleanor told him.

He shouted loudly for his father, and when there was no answer, he reluctantly let us in.

We were halfway across the courtyard when Paco's father came out.

"Good morning," he said.

"Good morning," Eleanor answered.

"What can I do for you?'

"I must speak with your mother."

The butcher narrowed his eyes. "My mother is old."

"This is an old story that I must discuss with her."

He looked at her inquiringly.

"It is about the house," she said.

"What about the house?"

"I want to discuss how she got it."

"Like everything else, with hard work." The butcher was growing less friendly with every exchange. "You have to come back another day, when my mother is home. She is at church."

"I'll wait for her," Eleanor insisted.

The butcher pointed to Tío's chair in the shade. "You can wait there."

Though it was hot and dusty in the courtyard, he left without offering us a drink. Eleanor took Tío's chair, and I sat on the ground.

"What if they don't come?" I asked after an hour had crawled by.

"They'll come."

The sun beat down on the courtyard, and the chickens wandered into the strip of shade by the north wall where we sat. Paco was nowhere to be seen.

Paco's grandmother didn't look happy to see us when she came through the door with his mother. Eleanor stood up to meet them, and Paco's father and brothers came out of the house and stood in a ring around us. Paco stood behind them.

"I have just come back from visiting Mr. Costa, the former bank manager of the *Caja de Ahorros.*" Eleanor paused, and they waited. The silence was charged. "His assistant manager came and visited you."

"No," Paco's grandmother said with finality.

"Yes," Eleanor pulled out a folded piece of paper. "Here is a letter confirming that he visited you in January, 1941."

Paco's grandmother wouldn't take the letter.

"No, no," she insisted. "I don't know anything about that letter. I don't know anything about that man. Whatever it says is a lie."

"The bank has all of the proof." Eleanor stayed calm.

Paco's mother took the letter and read it through. She looked at her husband. He held up his hands to stop her from saying anything.

"You bring this piece of garbage into the house...!" Paco's grandmother snatched the letter out of her daughter-in-law's hand and threw it on the ground.

"I want to see the deed to your house," Eleanor said firmly.

"The deed!!" Paco's father reacted as if she'd asked him to undress. "The deed is not for anyone's eyes! The deed is ours. The deed is nobody's business."

"There is a question about how you got it – the house was never sold by the Garcias."

"How we got the deed?!" The outrage was building. "You are senile, old woman. We have been here for decades. Everyone in the village saw us build this house with... with..." Paco's father held out his labourer's hands. "With our youth, with our children. We have built this. It is ours. You go. Foreigner. Old woman."

This was the final straw. Eleanor was angry. "You took this house from the Garcia family."

"You are lying!"

"You stoned Luis, an innocent boy, when he came home. Yes, you!!" She pointed at Paco's grandmother. "You started it all. Oh, I heard a few hints before everyone realized who I was and suddenly clammed up. I know you lost your brother, your favourite brother. He took you to all of the dances, introduced you to his best friend, who you ended up marrying."

"You see! She's been spying! I said that! I said that!" Paco's grandmother looked at her family as if she was presenting them with proof of Eleanor's wickedness.

"I came back to this village looking for the truth, nothing else," Eleanor defended herself. "You wanted revenge for your brother's life. You denounced Luis when he came back looking for his brother. You were angry and you lashed out at the first person you suspected was on the other side. You called him a Red, you shouted in the streets that he killed your brother. Almost everyone had lost someone. They were all full of grief and hate. It was easy for them to turn on Luis. They believed you. Everyone knew Alfonso was with the Reds, and you all assumed that Luis was too. But he had fought with the Nationals. With the same side as your brother."

Silence filled the courtyard like a fog.

Paco was looking at his grandmother with a pale face. I could see the confusion in his eyes and something else: shock, as if it occurred to him that his grandmother might not have told the truth.

Paco's grandmother was looking at Eleanor with murderous eyes. "You can't prove it."

"No," Eleanor admitted, "you went to Montilla and made sure of that. He had access to all the documents and he got rid of whatever he needed to. His signature was on everything. I'm sure he signed the property deed when you changed it into your name."

Paco's grandmother's mouth tightened in a worried line, and I knew Eleanor was right.

"I don't care about the property," she continued, turning to Paco's parents. "You're right. You've worked all your lives to build your business and raise your family here. I don't want the land back. What would I do with it?" She faced Paco's grandmother. "All I want now is to find Luis."

There was a staring match between Eleanor and Paco's grandmother, and the conversation between their eyes went deeper than words.

"This one action could make amends for what you did," Eleanor said. "This is your chance to make things right."

Paco's grandmother clenched her bulldog jaws. Her eyes were open, but it looked like they were closed by veils of darkness.

"I don't know what you're talking about," she said, before turning and walking away.

SIXTEEN

WE CROSSED BACK TO THE HOUSE, AND IT SEEMED to take forever in the hot, noon sun. I was crushed. How could this woman walk away from a horrible mistake she'd made? How could she deny everything when the truth was obvious?

"She's saving face," Eleanor said. "For some people, that is more important than anything else."

Amalia came in, and when she saw Eleanor's pale face, she scolded her for pushing herself too much. Eleanor must have been tired, because she allowed herself to be led to her room for a rest.

The day passed slowly and we were all restless. By siesta time, I couldn't bear the quiet in the house. I went up to the second floor and stepped out onto the balcony. I looked at Montilla's fortress across the square and I thought of the framed medals over his fireplace. His whole life he'd been a victorious conqueror, an authority that people feared and respected. Would he let anyone take that away from him?

Paco's front gate opened and he came out into the square. On impulse, I decided to go down and talk to him.

I hurried out the front door. The square was empty, and I could see no sign of him. I circled around, looking down the narrow streets that led off the square. They were all empty. The town was absolutely still during the siesta hour. It could have been the dead of night. I crossed by the passageway leading past Montilla's house, and that's where I caught sight of a figure just rounding the corner to the open field. Where was Paco going?

I hurried down the passageway. Paco knew the most surprising hiding places around the village. If I didn't hurry, he might disappear. I reached the field and stopped. He was nowhere in sight. A rustling of grass behind me made me turn around.

"What a surprise to find you out when the whole village is sleeping, Miss Garcia," said Montilla.

"I...I thought you were Paco."

"Haven't you been told to stay away from him?"

"It's something personal –"

"I don't think so," he cut me off. "I warned you before to mind your own business, you stupid, nosy child."

I tried to edge my way back towards the opening of the

passage, but he blocked me. His towering torso leaned forward. I looked behind me. The cliff face dropped a long way down. It wouldn't take much to slip and fall over the edge. My knees went weak.

"We know where my uncle is," I lied, but even as I said it, I knew it wouldn't make any difference.

His eyes narrowed, "What a shame that you won't get to meet him." He stepped towards me.

"Look out," I warned, stepping back, "I...I can outscream you, and...and...I can outrun you, and I...I can –"

I didn't get to finish the sentence, because his fingers clamped down on my left shoulder and dug in, hard as wood. It was too bad he didn't get to hear the last thing I could outdo him in, because everyone knows the best strategy in a fight is the element of surprise. Thank you, Ashley.

I swung my free arm, my right, forward, jabbing my fist hard – one, two – in his mouth and on his nose. I screamed with all my might, a warrior scream, and kicked his shin. "I can outbox you!"

He crumpled forward, holding his nose. I didn't wait a millisecond. My feet pounded down the passageway, and I burst out into the square yelling at the top of my lungs. Balcony doors were flung open, and Eleanor and Amalia came outside.

Montilla scrambled after me, limping and cursing, but I had already reached the safety of the house. Montilla stopped in the centre of the square. People surrounded him, looking at his bleeding nose and dishevelled hair.

"But even children now?" someone said. "Have shame!"

The villagers were silent. It felt like a wall was going up around the square, a wall that blocked Montilla and set him apart, on the outside. He looked shocked, as if he could feel his power seeping away from him. And when he turned to go into his house, he wasn't an officer any more, he was just an old man.

SEVENTEEN

O N SUNDAY, AMALIA AND I WERE UP EARLY PUTTING
together supplies for the churros when we heard a
soft knock on the front door. At first I thought it was
Amalia's knocking the bowls and utensils against the
counter, but then it came again, soft and persistent.

I walked across the patio and unlocked the iron gate. The
knocking stopped abruptly at the sound of the gate, and when
I opened the door, there was no one there. On the ground was
a small burlap bag, blackened with dirt, as if it had been
buried. I looked around the empty square. Paco peeked out
from behind the kiosk. I raised my hand in greeting. He raised
his hand back, then ran quickly to his house.

The bag rustled when I picked it up. I knew what was
in it. "It's Luis's papers!" I shouted, running through the
courtyard. "The ones he left at the bank!"

Eleanor hurried out of her bedroom, and Amalia ran across the square to put a sign on the stall announcing that it was closed. We cleared the dining room table and spread out the contents of the bag.

Luis had written on scraps of paper and in the margins of newspapers with a pencil. Because paper had been so scarce, his handwriting was tiny, sometimes looking like a series of dots and lines. Eleanor sent me to her study to get magnifying glasses and tweezers and cans of compressed air and brushes.

"Let's put these in some sort of order." Eleanor could barely contain herself. "Careful how you handle them, Ana. It looks like some of them are ready to disintegrate."

"He hasn't dated anything," I said, trying to decide where to start.

"He might not have known the date...maybe the newspaper scraps have dates," Eleanor guessed. "Yes! These three have dates."

We lifted them carefully – they were like big, yellow moth wings – and placed them gently in order.

"You start, Ana. Your eyes are the youngest."

I angled the magnifying glass until the tiny letters were in focus and moved it across the narrow column of writing in the margin of the newspaper:

The quiet is good. The quiet from people. People

*make a terrible noise. The wind makes a nice sound
and the grass when I walk through it. This is good
for my head. I have to hide, not even build a fire. I
stay in the caves like a shadow. I see other shadows
hiding too. Some go out when they shouldn't, when
they're too hungry to be careful, and they get caught
and taken away. I will wait for Alfonso and the
pretty Canadian.*

I looked up at Eleanor. "That's you?"

She nodded, her eyes brimming with silvery liquid in
the dim light.

I moved on to the next scrap of newspaper. A black
mould had bloomed across the page and covered the lines.

"I can't read it, Eleanor," I said.

"Try that soft brush there. See if you can remove it."
She watched me brush the paper gently. It picked up the
mould and left a lighter grey cloud on the paper that I
could read through.

*I am hungry. I can't make it go away. Every day it
grows stronger and I grow weaker. My belly feels like
an empty bowl. I eat some licorice root and thyme.
There were some wild figs, and in one hot corner,
prickly pears, but everything is picked clean. Dogs
are guarding the orchards and farm fields and I can't*

go near them. We are all after the same food. The villagers, the farmers, the soldiers, the people hiding. And there is nothing left.

"This is the last dated page here," I said, drawing it to me. Eleanor was looking out the window. "Do you want to stop?" I asked.

"I just wish Luis could have been spared this."

I waited.

"Alfonso's work made things dangerous for Luis. He sent me to get him, but the hospital wouldn't release him."

"Couldn't Luis escape to France like you did?"

"Alfonso and Luis were different. Alfonso was the more practical and confident of the two. He learned and adapted quickly. He picked up English and French...and he was good at getting information for his government."

"You mean he was a spy?!" I asked in surprise.

She nodded. "And Luis, on the other hand, was a dreamer. He didn't understand what was happening and didn't care about the movement of military lines. It probably didn't occur to him to try to leave Spain when he got out of the hospital. He just thought Alfonso and I would come back for him when the war was over. Go on, read," she urged me.

The sun is changing and I know that winter is

coming. Rain has started and the cave is cold. I have no blanket. How will I get through the winter without a fire? I have to go to the bank where we have the family papers. Maybe there is a message for me there. Maybe there is some money there. I can't sit here anymore. If I keep shivering like this, I will shake everything loose inside me.

"Mr. Costa must have seen him at the bank a couple of days after this!"

"Yes!" Eleanor agreed. "Maybe these come next." She laid out scraps of paper, wrappers from cigarette packages that had writing on the back, a train ticket, a release slip from a hospital. "Look here! He was released from the hospital on January 12, 1939." She turned the slip over and there was writing on the back.

They hate me. They attacked me and called me a traitor, a dog. The cold is too much to bear. Where are you, brother?

"Why couldn't you get in touch with him?" I asked.

"We were exiles, and there was no information coming across to us. We listened on the short-wave to Spanish radio, but all they played for months after Franco won was the national anthem or speeches about the greatness of Franco and his power. It was hard to make contact with any of the people left in Spain, because short-wave radios were illegal and no one dared be found with one. We were completely out of touch." She put the hospital release slip aside regretfully. "What else is there?"

We sifted through the papers. "There must be more here!" Eleanor said. She picked up a newspaper clipping with no writing on it and threw it aside.

"What was that?" I asked.

"It didn't have anything on it."

"No, what does the headline say?"

Eleanor brought her glasses to her face, then lifted her eyes to me.

"Well done!" she exclaimed.

"What is it?"

"*Anti-Franco Nest Discovered in Sierra.* It's about Alfonso and Luis," her voice was incredulous, "doing war crimes against Paco's grandmother!??" She sped through the article, mumbling to herself, then speaking aloud at the important parts. "...*Luis and Alfonso Garcia are known enemies of the state and the police are following several leads and anticipate an arrest soon!!...(mumble, mumble)...in light of their crimes against Graciela Sanchez and family, the village of Sierra, and the state, their rights as property owners are being withdrawn, and, in compensation for her suffering and for her support of the state in reporting the activities of* the brothers, *Graciela Sanchez will take possession of and full responsibility for the property they abandoned in their criminal pursuits!"*

"There it is! Proof!" I shouted. "Proof! Proof!"

Amalia wanted to march across the square right away.

"Wait! We're close now. Let's see what comes of this!" said Eleanor. There were only a few papers left to read. She handed me one written in tight, neat lines. "Read this."

I keep thinking of my last contact with Alfonso. It was through the Canadian. She brought fresh sheets and food and checked my medicine. We talked about Alfonso. I knew she loved him. I slept and woke and she was still there. She told me stories about Montreal, the city she comes from where they speak French and English and they have a quantity of good food and cafés. And they drink milk in the morning. That's all I remember, and even if it was a dream, it is the only dream I have. Because Canada is where Consuelo is, so first I will find her and then together we will find Alfonso.

Eleanor was dumbfounded. "Of all the places in the world, I didn't think to look in Canada."

EIGHTEEN

Eleanor set to work once she had a fresh trail to follow. We went to Madrid, where we visited the Canadian consulate to try to find Luis in Canada. We found a company that was called People Finders, and they started looking in Montreal. I was surprised when, a few days later, we had a name, telephone number, and address in Quebec.

Eleanor was caught off guard by the suddenness of finding Luis. She sat for a day with the paper in her hand, and then she tucked it away somewhere and did nothing for another couple of days.

"Did you throw the number away?" I finally confronted her.

"No," she answered mildly.

"Well?"

She breathed in and out. "I...it's been so long...and I don't know who I will find. Will he be glad to hear from me? Will he be healthy and happy? I suppose I wasn't prepared for this, that's all."

"So will you call?"

She sighed and didn't answer.

"Will you call before I leave?" I pressed.

She finally nodded her head and instructed me to get the paper. "It's in my study, in the cubicle beside the tweezers."

I fetched it quickly and sat beside her while she dialed. Amalia came into the room to dust things that didn't need dusting. I could hear the faint long-distance rings in the receiver, and my stomach turned jittery with nerves.

"Hello...?" Eleanor said and hesitated. "Yes...is this Luis Garcia, brother of Alfonso, from Sierra, Spain?"

I heard a faint exclamation, then Eleanor started laughing, while her eyes brimmed with tears. "I've been looking for you for a long time!... Yes, it's Eleanor.... Yes, the Canadian."

Amalia had stopped pretending to clean and was crying loudly into her handkerchief.

The telephone conversation was short. They were both so shocked to hear from each other that they seemed at a loss for words, and yet had so much to say that they kept speaking over each other.

When Eleanor hung up, I asked, "Well?"

"Have you ever seen Montreal, Ana?"

"No."

"We'll have to change that." She laughed and her eyes sparkled. "Will you come with me to meet him?"

"Sure!!"

I HAD A FEW THINGS TO WRAP UP IN SIERRA. I asked Eleanor who the motorbike belonged to.

"It's yours, of course," she told me.

"Then I can do what I want with it?"

"Certainly."

On the day I was leaving, I got up early and wheeled my motorbike out into the deserted square. I waited behind the kiosk until Paco's door opened and he slipped out with his package of sausages for Montilla. As he was running back to his house, I stepped out and hissed, "Pssst."

He turned around, surprised to see me.

I pushed the motorbike over to him. "Aren't you sick of jumping off the back of the truck every time your brothers drive you to school?" He looked guarded and didn't answer me. "I'm not teasing you," I said. "Here," I held the bike out to him. "For next year."

He looked at it, mouth open. *"Para mi?"*

"Yes, for you."

He grabbed the handlebars and got on, grinning. "Come for a ride?"

We rolled down the hill with the engine off until we reached the bottom, where he brought the motor to life and we drove into the hills. I wondered if we'd talk about everything that had happened between his family and mine. I thought about saying something, but it was hard to put my feelings into words, and in the end we just sat at the lookout point that jutted over the valley and watched the sun come up.

When Pepe's taxi skidded to a stop in front of the house, Antonio and Amalia helped us get our bags into the trunk. Amalia's eyes were red, and she fussed with my ponytail and made a great deal of fuss about adjusting the strap on Eleanor's purse so it was just the right length. When we drove away, Amalia alternated between waving her handkerchief in the air and wiping her eyes with it. She was staying in the village. Eleanor had given her and Antonio the house as a wedding present.

Halfway down the hill, I saw Cricket jumping up and down.

"Stop, Pepe!" I shouted.

Pepe complained good-naturedly as we came to a squealing stop. I dug down into the bottom of my flight bag to find the change purse I'd buried there with souvenir *pesetas*.

"Here, Cricket!" I tossed the change purse to him. "That's for three extra-large orders."

He cheered as if he'd just won the world cup and ran after the taxi until we hit the dirt road at the bottom of the village, where he disappeared in the wake of dust behind us.

I LOOKED AT MY WATCH. IT WAS 5:00 P.M. The plane banked, and I got my first glimpse of Montreal sparkling in the afternoon sunlight. Eleanor had changed my return ticket so I could fly with her to Montreal. It was funny how the end of this mystery was making the beginning of a whole new story. Eleanor said I had many Garcia cousins, and some of them would meet us at the airport. My mother was coming too. My father had a new job and had to stay in Toronto until the weekend. I didn't know what Eleanor was expecting, but I was picturing a huge family reunion with fireworks and music.

When we landed, it seemed to take forever for the passengers to get their things from the overhead compartments, and then we walked in an unbearably slow line down the aisle of the airplane and out to customs.

I realized how much I'd missed my mother when I saw her at the exit gate. I dropped my suitcase and charged into her arms.

"Hello, Aunt Eleanor," my mother said, after I finally

released her. They hugged, and I was surprised to hear Eleanor say that the last time she'd seen my mother she'd been a skinny little girl.

"Hey, Canadian," a soft voice said behind our backs.

Eleanor turned around. A man with black hair streaked with white stood with such a glow of happiness on his face that it looked as if there was an electric light under his skin.

"Luis!" Eleanor exclaimed. "You're here!" They hugged, then stood apart and examined each other in wonderment.

"They wanted me to wait at home, while they picked you up," he pointed to a smiling couple behind him, "and I said, 'No! I've been waiting too long.'" He beamed at her.

"You must meet your niece! This is Consuelo's daughter, Marta," Eleanor said, introducing my mother.

"You don't know how long I looked for your mother in Montreal, but...well, I didn't have a clue where to find her," he said with regret. He turned to me. "And is this the girl?"

"Yes, this is Ana. The one who led the way to you," Eleanor said, in a way that made me feel I would float happily off the ground.

Luis introduced his daughter, Margarita, and her husband, John. "There was only room for one of my grandchildren in the car, but the others are waiting," he said, looking around. "Where is Rocio?"

I watched Margarita and my mother bend their heads together to talk.

"Rocio! Come meet your cousin," Luis called.

Rocio, a girl no more than four years old, was seated in a waiting area behind us. Her hands and face were covered with crumbs and splotches of honey and peanut butter.

"Hello," she cried and puckered her lips for a kiss. I waved from a safe distance.

As we left the airport, I looked at Luis and thought of everything that he'd survived. His eyes were gentle and happy, as if a good life had erased the hard times he'd had in Spain when he was young.

In the parking lot, Rocio puckered her lips at me again. When our suitcases were loaded in the minivan, I noticed she'd already planted several sticky lip marks on Eleanor's suitcase and I chose my seat carefully, making sure I was far enough away that she couldn't demand a kiss.

DINNER WAS OVER. The living room was filled with red faces from the heat in the kitchen where a wide black stove had produced a mountain of food for all of us, including Luis's five children and twelve grandchildren.

We were all pleasantly stuffed, and settled in couches and chairs and on the floor to listen to Eleanor and Luis. One or two of the grown-ups snored contentedly.

"There are too many years to fill in, in such a short time," my mother complained to Eleanor and Luis.

They both laughed.

"Now we'll have lots of time to talk," Luis said.

"And I'm coming back home to Canada," Eleanor sighed and leaned back in her seat. "Finally."

"So tell us!" Margarita said impatiently.

Eleanor looked at Luis. "You start."

"I was drafted into the army, I remember, on...now what day was it, the 23rd or the 24th?"

"It doesn't matter grandpa, just tell the story!" his grandson, Paul, shouted.

"They want the short version," Eleanor muttered to him.

They exchanged a look of understanding.

"I was drafted when I was seventeen years old. My dear mother was very sick and we lived with her sister who had a bakery that made horrible bread – out of rice flour and other such things, because there was little wheat flour – but we ate it gratefully. I went into the army so there would be one less mouth to feed and because we had to register as residents so that my mother could get medical treatment. I was in the army for no more than a year before I got malaria and was too sick to fight."

"Did you kill anyone?" Paul wanted to know.

"I was not a warrior, Pauly. I didn't have the hatred in my gut that some of the men did. I was too busy thinking of my mother and my friend, Flaco, who was a year younger than me and hungrier than a bear because he was growing so fast. And we just did our work, ate our meals, and slept – when we could. In the winter it rained, and always, at some point in the night, there was a leak at my head. So I had to sleep with my pillow wet and my head hanging off the cot."

"It sounds gross," exclaimed Angela, his granddaughter who was my age.

"Eleanor was there," Luis said, turning to her. "She knows too."

"Oh yes, I was a volunteer nurse. Half the time our trucks broke down and we couldn't get supplies out to the lines. The hardest thing was keeping things clean and making small areas sterile, you know, because Madrid was under attack all the time.

"I met a lot of fine people over there. There were a lot of Canadians from the Mackenzie-Papineau Battalion, and Americans from the Abraham Lincoln Battalion, and British, Irish, and French people. Really, volunteers came from around the world to fight for the people of Spain. That was where I met Alfonso, Luis, and Consuelo's older brother.

"Alfonso was doing dangerous work for the Republicans – and he was terribly worried when he found out that Luis was in the National army." She turned to Luis. "He was afraid that if they found out you were his brother, the Civil Guard might think you were working with him and kill you."

Luis shook his head. "I had no idea...."

"That was why he sent me to get you when he found out you were in hospital," Eleanor continued. "He got me fake papers and I went to see you. We thought that if I could get you out, I could take care of you while we travelled. You were very weak, and you slipped in and out of a fever while I was there. The hospital refused to let me take you. And I didn't want to raise suspicion by making a scene. I stayed as long as I could, to see if you would improve, but after two days I had to leave. I didn't think that you would remember me or what I talked about."

"But yes!" Luis exclaimed. "You told me about Montreal and the bagels."

"The bagels!" everyone shouted.

"And the cafés, and the music, and skating on ice, and the river!" he continued.

"So what happened when you were released from the hospital?" Eleanor asked.

"They sent me back to fight. But I couldn't go back. I knew I would never shoot a gun." Luis shook his head. "So I ran."

"You deserted?" I asked.

"Yes," he said, "and then I went back to the village to look for Alfonso." He looked at Eleanor. "It's funny what fever does. I remembered your visit and what you said about Montreal, but I don't remember where you said Alfonso would be."

"That's because I didn't tell you. I couldn't risk it, for both your safety and his."

Luis nodded. "The only place I could think to look for him was at home. But when I got there, the villagers accused me of being a Red. It was Graciela who started it. She was always a nasty busybody, even as a girl. When she saw me, she started shrieking as if I had marched into the square and started gunning people down. She called me a traitor and said I had murdered her brother and half of the men in the village.

"People came out of their houses, and I could see the hatred in their eyes, and when they saw me, they started throwing whatever they had in their hands – garbage, sticks, stones. I ran, and they chased me."

"Oh, Papa, that's horrible," said Margarita sadly.

"Yes, but I was lucky. The goatherder who lived in the hills around the village found me and took me to his home until my injuries healed."

Eleanor said, "Alfonso felt guilty for the way we fled Spain. He always said that he abandoned you, and that if he could have reached you before the end, you would have come to safety with us."

"But it was as difficult for you in exile as it was for me in Spain," he said gently, and continued. "The goatherder started hearing gossip that the *Guardia* were asking for me in the village. The authorities wanted me because I was a deserter, and the villagers reported that I was a Red, which made it even worse. I was better, and since it was no longer safe for him to hide me, we decided I should go.

"I remembered some caves that were small and difficult to get to that Alfonso had showed me. They were his secret childhood place, and I went to live there. Every once in a while, the goatherder brought me some goat milk or cheese, otherwise I would have starved. The little news that I got from the scraps of newspaper that he wrapped his cheese in told me that Franco had won and Spain was becoming a land I didn't know.

"After a few months of waiting in the caves and watching the road for Alfonso, I started to lose hope. As a last resort, I decided to travel to Toledo and go to the bank where we had a safety deposit box, hoping to find money or a message there. When I saw my reflection in the green glass door of the bank, I didn't recognize myself. I had long hair and my clothes were dirty. I was frightened by my appearance and knew how dangerous it was for me to be out in public. I knew I should have just looked for what I needed and left, but I found the deed to the house with my parents' signature and I stayed with the papers, as if I was visiting with my family. And I left my notes in that box, as if I was talking to them.

"When I came out, the clerk jumped on my back and tried to wrestle me to the ground. I kicked at him and finally got away. I didn't know where to go, and I couldn't make myself go back to the caves, so once again, I went to the goatherder.

"The good man didn't want anything to do with me. He was afraid now. Things were much tougher, and the *Guardia* were ruthless with anyone they suspected of being against Franco. But he couldn't turn me away cold.

"He took a razor and cut my hair and shaved me and gave me one of his jackets. This for him was a huge gift. He had only one jacket left for himself and would not be able to get another for years. Then he pointed to the west and said five days of walking would take me to Portugal, where there were many boats. They didn't like Spanish exiles, though. Or, he pointed north, I could walk seven days and get to France through a mountain range they said was like spears of death. I decided to go west.

"I hid in the first big ship that I found in Portugal. I was so afraid that they would turn around and bring me back that I stayed in my hiding place until I fainted."

"Papa! You're crazy!" Margarita shouted.

He held up his hand to calm her down. "Happily, someone found me. The boat was heading for Cuba, and they made good use of me. I worked hard and earned my passage. Once in Cuba, I made my way slowly to Canada. It was during World War II and there was work in factories everywhere I went. It took me two years to cross the United States and come to Canada. By that time, I had learned a bit of English. I came to Montreal to find my sister, Consuelo, but she was with Eleanor's family and I didn't know their family name, and in the end, I lost hope of ever finding her."

Then it was Eleanor's turn, and she explained how she and Alfonso had fled to France, then Belgium, and had worked in the diamond business. She described their search for Luis all over Spain and through international agencies. She explained that Consuelo had married and moved to Toronto.

My mother explained that when Abuela died, she left a plane ticket for me. Eleanor talked about my visit, and I described my conversation with the goatherder. There was cheering and clapping as we came to the climax of our story. When we finished talking, it was late. Margarita brewed coffee and then big plates of cakes were passed around.

ELEANOR RETURNED TO SPAIN to pack up the house and finish business there. She had decided to get the goatherder a new jacket, to replace the one his father had given Luis so many years ago. She promised to write, and a few weeks after she left, I received a thick letter in the mail. Inside was a picture framed in stiff card with a cover. When I opened the cover, I screamed.

There I was on my hands and knees, eyes popping in fear, mouth open, hair sticking out as if I'd just received an electric shock. It was me in the cave where Luis had lived. Eleanor must have developed the film in the camera I'd had around my wrist when I was crawling around and accidentally took a picture. On the back of the frame, Eleanor had written:

You may be too young to appreciate this photo, but I have framed it and placed in my gallery of heroes.

I closed the cover and put the picture in the bottom of my dresser drawer. I only hoped her gallery of heroes wasn't a place she gave tours of.

ACKNOWLEDGEMENTS

Thanks to my father, who so willingly shared his stories about the civil war with me, to my mother for her unwavering support, and to my brother, Sandy, who taught me how to ride a motorbike on the back roads of Benalmadena, Spain.

ABOUT THE AUTHOR

Diana Vazquez studied film and video at the Ontario College of Art and has spent several years writing and producing her own short and independent dramas and experimental films. Her first juvenile fiction novel, *Hannah*, was published by Coteau Books in 1999.

Born in Germany, to Israeli and Spanish parents, Diana Vazquez moved many times with her family before settling in Canada. Her passion for reading sustained her through these many disruptions. The birth of her own daughter rekindled her interest in children's books, and she now spends more time writing than filmmaking.